Theaker's Quarterly Fiction #53

Edited by
Stephen Theaker
and John Greenwood

Theaker's Quarterly Fiction #53

Edited by
Stephen Theaker
and John Greenwood

Cover Artist

Howard Watts

Contributors

Allen Ashley
Douglas J. Ogurek
Howard Watts
Jacob Edwards
Mitchell Edgeworth

Contents

Editorial

Fiction

The Quarterly Review

CONTENTS

Games

Music

Television

Notes

Editorial

Stephen Theaker

Thanks for picking up a copy of this much-delayed issue of our magazine! This was supposed to be out last September, but I got sidetracked and ended up helping out on two issues of *BFS Horizons* for the British Fantasy Society. I've actually produced five of their last seven publications now, and bit by bit that's led to you, my dear darlings, my Theakery friends, being neglected. I'm very sorry! This year I'll be putting you first.

Apologies as well to fans of our regular ongoing serials from Walt Brunston, Antonella Coriander and Howard Phillips, squeezed out of this issue and the next (which will be out very soon too, and contains a complete novella by BFS short story competition winner Patrick Whittaker). They will be back in issue 55 or 56, with the next instalments of each saga: "With Echoing Feet He Threaded", "This Alien I" and "The Little Shop That Sold My Heart", respectively.

News broke this week that the Spectral Press, a very active UK horror small press, has run into trouble, with debts of £8,000 owing and pre-ordered books not having been printed or shipped. It's a shame whenever this happens. In this case it looks like a case of too much, too soon, with a successful run of chapbooks leading to an expansion into signed and limited hardbacks that possibly came too soon.

While very sad, it's given me renewed admiration for those small presses that do keep going, the Gray Friars, the PS Publishings, the TTA Presses. Every time I've dipped a publishing toe in those waters I've caught quite a chill, so that they manage to keep doing it year after year is nothing short of amazing. And props as well to the newcomers, like Fox Spirit Books and *Holdfast Magazine*, who seem to be doing so much right.

We have three super stories for you this time. In "Restitution" Mitchell Edgeworth takes us back to the *Black Swan*, its crew double-crossed by the thief Nisha. In "Dodge Sidestep's (and Martin's) Final Dastardly Plan" our regular cover artist Howard Watts completes his absurdist musical trilogy. And "Rathfern's Menagerie" is a bodyswapping science fantasy from Allen Ashley. I think you'll enjoy all of them – and our fifty pages of reviews too! I went through a phase last year of writing a review a day, while Douglas and Jacob have been as productive as ever. (And somewhat more in-depth!)

So once again, my apologies to our readers, and our contributors, for all the delays. But now they are over. And it is time for you to read. Please do so!

Stephen Theaker's reviews have appeared in Black Static, Interzone, Prism and the BFS Journal, as well as clogging up our pages. He shares his home with three slightly smaller Theakers, runs the British Fantasy Awards, and works in legal and medical publishing.

Restitution

Black Swan #7

Mitchell Edgeworth

Captain Keiji Duval of the *Black Swan* woke in his cabin one morning to the sight of a bizarre golden tube slanted above his bed. It took him a moment, blinking and squinting as he emerged from the kingdom of sleep, to realise that it was light: actual daylight, streaming in through the porthole. Keiji had spent far longer repairing the ancient, fifth-hand shell of the *Swan* than he yet had skippering her as a legitimately spaceworthy vessel. Every time she made landfall and he woke to bright light and silence and utter stillness, he sleepily thought it was the old days again, back in the junkyard on Mars, just him and the ship.

He watched dust motes drift through the light for a moment before sitting up, peering out the porthole and trying to remember where they were. Squinting through the glare he could make out brightly lit wheat fields and dusty plains, a ruffle of cedar trees in the creases between distant hills. Corduba, that was it. A C-type asteroid. One of the bigger settled worlds in the main belt, so large that it actually let small vessels like the *Swan* fly right on inside and land on the interior surface. Spanish-speaking, a pampas biome dotted with hundreds of farms and cattle ranches, broken up by hills and forests and centring on a large town on the shores of a lake.

Keiji lay back down in bed, stretching and yawning, flicking his netlinks on to fill his eyes and ears with media: local breakfast news in Spanish, a jaunty advertising jingle, disembodied voices and sounds rattling around in his brain. He could switch to translation if he liked, but he enjoyed doing this when he landed on a new world: exposing himself to unfamiliar languages and accents, savouring a sense of exoticism. It was 8.35 am on Corduba, a rare case of shipboard time and landside time more or less synching up, and Keiji felt optimistic about the day ahead.

There was a knock at the cabin door. "Yeah?"

The *Black Swan*'s first mate, Chase, poked his head in. "Nisha's gone."

Keiji frowned, sitting up again. "What do you mean, gone?" Nisha was an associate from a former job that had gone badly, a professional thief whom Keiji had technically screwed over. As way of penance he'd helped her escape Jupiter before she could come to grief at the hands of her would-be clients, and she'd been aboard the *Black Swan* for the past six weeks as they island-hopped across the asteroid belt.

"I mean she's gone. Cabin's empty. Cleared out her stuff, took her bag."

"What?" Keiji said. "No way, man. She was just starting to settle in. She probably just went for a walk. You know how cooped up she feels here."

"All her stuff is gone," Chase repeated.

Keiji kicked his sheets aside and pulled on his jeans. "As if she even has that much stuff. She'll be back this afternoon. You got a pot of coffee going?"

Chase was avoiding eye contact. "Uh... Keiji..."

"What?"

"She took the cargo."

The galley's exhaust fan had been broken for a long time, and cooking breakfast was an activity typically performed within a shroud of white smoke. Chase cracked a few more eggs into a dangerously overcrowded frying pan and glanced through the haze at Keiji. The captain was already on his second coffee, looking out the galley porthole at Corduba's main city, Cascade.

"You reckon she's in town?" Chase asked.

"She must be." Keiji stared across the farmland at the distant city, a picturesque cluster of white Mediterranean buildings at the edge of the lake. The wind was rippling across golden fields of wheat, the shadows of puffy clouds scudding across the landscape. "Where else would she go?"

"Bit of a walk," said Kingsford, the ship's pilot.

"For all we know she left before midnight," Keiji said. "Or got a taxi. Or, shit, maybe she nicked the jeep as well." He'd meant the last one as a joke, but then he hesitated and turned to Chase. "You *did* check..."

"The jeep's still there," Chase said. "Jesus, give me a little credit."

Keiji took a seat at the tiny table, waving smoke out of his face. "Well, anyway, there's nothing else out here but farms and grassland. She definitely went into the city."

"Okay, so she's in the city," Chase said, shovelling the fry-up onto their plates and slathering his own with an alarming amount of barbecue sauce. "How do we find that particular needle in the haystack?"

"Maybe we should call the police," Kingsford said. Chase and Keiji stared at him across the table. "What? You said this was a legal cargo. You were very proud of that."

The cargo in question was ninety-six gengineered cattle embryos – Cimmerian Angus with a strain of

authentic Terran Pajuna, to be precise – in a vacuum
flask that could fit inside a briefcase. It was a private
delivery from a Corduban expat Keiji had met on
Nuevo Navarre, to be delivered back home to his
cousin, one of the asteroid's premier cattle ranchers.
Or so he'd said at a restaurant on Nuevo Navarre,
going into great detail about Corduban politics and
the ranching rivalries and blah blah blah. Keiji had
already been on his third glass of wine by that point,
and was fixated on the payment.

"It is legal," Keiji said. "Perfectly legal. But failing to
declare it at customs wasn't. If we get caught we'll have
to pay the import fees, and a fine on top of that, and
it'll make the whole venture pointless. So no police."

"That's not legal, then," Kingsford said. "It's
smuggling. You... you *know* that."

"Oh, whatever."

"Maybe we could list her as a missing person," Chase
said. "Not officially, I mean. Just flood the net with it.
'Have you seen our missing crewmember,' that kind of
thing. Grassroots search campaign."

"No. The cops would get wind of it anyway."

"So what's your plan, then?" Kingsford said.

"I don't know. I guess we head down to Cascade and
look around for her."

"What, just wander the streets?" Kingsford said.
"And what do you mean, 'we'?"

Keiji frowned. "Are you a member of this crew, or
aren't you?"

"I'm a pilot," Kingsford said, getting up and scraping
the remains of his breakfast into the bin. "I fly the
ship. I'm not your truant officer."

"You can't..."

"I can't what? Where in my contract does it say that
it's my job to help clean up the consequences of your
mistakes?"

"You don't *have* a contract! And what do you think you're saying? This is *my* fault?"

Kingsford glanced at Chase, who looked uneasy. "He has a point, man," the first mate said. "What happened on Ganymede... well. You might want to cut your losses on this one and call it square."

Keiji stared across the table at his crew. "I can't believe I'm hearing this."

"Look," Kingsford said, "do what you want, but I'm too old to go traipsing around on some sun-baked Spanish rock looking for your runaway floozy."

"She's *not* a floozy, whatever that is, and you're – what, sixty?"

"I'm sixty-seven," Kingsford glared. "And you should have left her on Ganymede. Enjoy your wild goose chase." The old man stalked out of the galley.

Chase shifted uncomfortably in his chair. "Like I said. He sort of has a point."

"Put your shoes on," Keiji said. "Let's go."

Chase found the Black Swan's *living room – or "mess", as Keiji insisted they call it – deeply comforting. With the ship's cabins the size of matchboxes, it was natural that they spent most of their spare time in the mess, sunk in the couches and armchairs, knocking back beers and smoking joints. Net reception between worlds was shaky at best and slow anyway, but the ship's computer had an enormous backlog of three centuries' worth of film and television, and Chase spent many of his interplanetary days with his ass parked on the couch in front of the screen. For someone who'd grown up in the freezing slums of Agassiz and then spent most of his adulthood running from one deadly thing or another, it was a refreshing change. There was something womblike about it: warm and entertained, in a fug of alcohol and marijuana, ferried between worlds in the guts of small and cosy vessel.*

Until Nisha came. She spent as much time in the mess as anyone, calling her cabin a "coffin," but it was clear she felt claustrophobic anywhere on the ship. She paced up and down the halls and was constantly staring out the portholes at the motionless stars. Chase could hear her moving about the ship when he was in bed. When they'd landed on Blomanda and she'd rejected it as an exit point because it was too close to Jupiter, she'd asked how long until their next destination. When Keiji had told her it was seven days to High Brazil – by no means a long haul in the tramp freighting trade – she'd blanched. But she'd stayed.

Chase couldn't help but feel some sympathy from her. He knew all too well that chronic anxiety, that ever-present fear of shadowy forces over your shoulder. But he couldn't understand why she still carried that knot of stress and anxiety with her to the Black Swan. *He'd felt nothing but relief after going off-world. Chase thought of the Swan a sanctuary, not a prison.*

It took time, he supposed. It was only a few weeks since her life had been turned upside down. After his own cataclysm he'd been a mess for years. Everything, in the end, was just a matter of time.

Cascade took its name from the water. Corduba's architects had designed the main river so that upon reaching the city it split into thousands of smaller waterways. Canals, brooks and streams gurgled through the streets like a spiderweb, parting and joining, traversing waterfalls and fountains and ornamental ponds, narrowing and widening, until they finally reunited at the harbour and poured into the lake. Nearly every street was flanked with little channels no more than a foot wide, so no matter where you stood in Cascade you were never more than a few metres away from running water. It was quite pretty, Keiji thought, to follow the flow downhill through the labyrinthine streets of the central medina, crossing hundreds of little bridges, before eventually emerging along the city's main avenue, Romanos Rambla.

It was also hot and tiring. Corduba's spin put the gravity at .8 g, which was more than twice what Keiji's Martian frame was accustomed to. He stopped by a gurgling stream and sat on a stone bench in the shade of a weeping willow to catch his breath. He tilted his head back to look up through the leaves. On most asteroids you could quite plainly see the other side of the interior, only a few kilometres away, whether it was a city or fields or an ocean or anything. Corduba, though, was so huge that the far side was virtually invisible, lost in the swirling centrifugal clouds, past the glare of the faux-suns strung in a line across the gravity spine.

Keiji sighed, and checked his map again. He was almost there. He turned to watch the traffic cruising along Romanos Rambla: bicycles, pedestrians, a charmingly antique tram. Born and bred in heavy g, strolling along without a care in the world. And Earth had been a full 1 g. The mind boggled. He hauled himself to his feet again and trudged across the road.

By noon Chase had long since abandoned the fruitless search and was at a bar down on the lakeside, sitting at a wooden table beneath a beach umbrella, drinking and smoking and watching sailboats out on the water. It was still sunny in Cascade, but there was a summer storm brewing out over the lake, on the sternward side of the asteroid, patiently inching towards the town. The boats were reluctantly trimming back towards the marina, and a waitress was folding up and taking inside the umbrellas from the unoccupied tables. Down by the jetties, children were still shrieking and running and cannonballing into the water. The air was pregnant with humidity.

It was an impressive sight, watching a storm coagulate in Corduba. Like most asteroids, it was built on the O'Neill principle, a hollowed-out cylinder in which the inhabitants lived on the inside surface, centrifugal force providing an approximation of gravity. At ground level this process was indistinguishable from being on a planet, apart from the obvious fact that you could typically look up and see the other side of your little world looking back at you. But in the air, the closer you went to the middle, the lighter the gravity was. So the clouds formed up near the gravity spine, a roiling and ominous mass enveloping the faux-suns, flickering with lightning, and as it began to rain the water fell in a spiralling pattern, coiling around the centre, picking up weight and speed before eventually lashing diagonally down into the lake. It was a genuinely breathtaking sight, and Chase figured he still had time to appreciate it with another pint of Sol de Mayo and a third cigarette before the storm reached him.

His computer trilled and Keiji's ID picture came up: a photo Chase had taken of him while he was sloppily eating an ice cream. Chase sighed and let it ring for a moment before answering. "Yeah?"

"*Where are you?*"

"Just working my way down the third barrio," Chase said. "Near the marina, like you said."

"*Yeah? How's the beer?*"

"I'm not..." Chase looked up and down the waterfront, which was still crowded with people in spite of the coming storm. A gelato vendor extolled his treats with a hearty Latin bellow, and the music of competing buskers clashed across opposite sides of the promenade. "Are you watching me?"

"No. Call it an educated guess. Anyway, come have lunch with me. I'll send you the address."

"Given up as well, huh?"

"No. I'm just pretty sure I know where she is."

El Gato Negro. A tapas bar at the edge of Cascade's medina, nestled in an cavernous cellar with a brick-vaulted ceiling, the walls lined with oak barrels of port. One of the city's streams had been diverted underground here, running through a channel in the floor before arriving in an enormous pond at the far end, koi circling endlessly beneath the lily pads. It was busy for the lunch hour, three quarters full, with conversations in Spanish drifting amid the clink of wine glasses and the clatter of cutlery on plates. Chase descended the wooden steps into the cellar just as the first raindrops began spattering on the cobblestones outside, and soon found Keiji in a far corner, drinking coffee and eating olives.

"Don't order anything alcoholic," Keiji said, before Chase had even sat down. "We might be here for a while and I need you sober."

"I think it's offensive you assume I'll automatically want a drink," Chase said, picking up a menu. "But, also, you know, I feel compelled to point out they do jugs of sangria for twenty pesos."

"You can drink as much as you want once this is over. Be a big boy and show some professionalism for once in your life."

"I'm plenty professional." Chase flagged down a waiter, mangled the pronunciation of *cimarron*, and ordered a few tapas plates. "So. What's the deal?"

"Well," Keiji said, "it's probably occurred to you that the only reason Nisha took off now is because we had a cargo small enough for her to physically pick up and walk away with."

"The thought had crossed my mind."

"But she doesn't know anybody here. She doesn't have contacts. She can't take it off-world. So who's she going to sell it to?" Keiji leaned back in his chair, looking smug. "The same people we were going to deliver it to. She's got no other options."

Chase's coffee arrived and he dropped a few sugar cubes in it, to the waiter's naked contempt. "That doesn't make sense. How would she know who that is?"

"Well," Keiji said. "You know. She's *wily*, and all that. She probably lifted it from my computer."

"How would she get access to your computer?"

Keiji looked out across the restaurant, avoiding Chase's eyes. "She... well, she might have been in my cabin a few times."

Chase clapped his hands together, suddenly delighted. "I *knew* it! I fucking knew it!" He laughed. "I knew something was up this morning, when you were all, 'oh, she must have gone for a walk'. A fucking walk. *Please*. You had this coming, man. You so had this coming."

"How?" Keiji demanded.

"Oh, come on," Chase grinned. "All that crap back at Jupiter? You owed her and you know it. And then you let her honeypot you! Admit it. Ha! This is too good."

"That was different," Keiji said. "This isn't *my* cargo. It belongs to the rancher. We're just the delivery boys."

"It wasn't *your* cargo to steal back from her on Ganymede, either," Chase pointed out, spearing an olive with a toothpick.

"It wasn't hers to steal in the first place!" Keiji hissed. "This is different. This is the duly purchased property of one businessman, being supplied to his cousin, *also* a legitimate businessman. No theft involved."

"Right. Just smuggling."

"This is a legitimate cargo," Keiji said stubbornly. "A delivery. Made on behalf of two honest entrepreneurs, trying to... you know, trying to get around the unjust tariffs and import taxes of a bullying government."

Chase laughed again. "I know for a fact you vote Social Democrat."

"Look, whatever. I'm not angry at her. If it was my own money I might let it go, so we could call it square. But it's not my cargo to give up."

"Yessss," Chase said, sucking his teeth, "*although*, you have to admit, she was in hot water back on Ganymede as well. You took something away from her that she was supposed to give to her clients. And they seemed a bit more dangerous than some cattle rancher on a backwater asteroid."

"Well, anyway, it doesn't matter," Keiji said. "Because – if we could get back to the business at hand for a moment – she's almost definitely going to take it to the same drop point."

"Let me guess," Chase said, trying to work a piece of olive skin out of his teeth. "This is the drop point."

"Yep."

"So how do we know she didn't drop it off already?"

"It doesn't open till noon, and I've been here since then."

Chase raised an eyebrow. "That's a bit, uh..." He snapped a toothpick in half, and continued rummaging around in his teeth. "How do you know she didn't just knock on the door early?"

"Look, I didn't think of it before," Keiji said. "Christ, for all I know she isn't even planning to sell it. Maybe she tossed it in the sewer just to get back at me."

"Doubt it. Not her style."

Keiji drained the last of his coffee, stared at the olive

pits clustered in their porcelain bowl. "Maybe. I don't know. We don't really know her, do we?"

Nisha entered the flight deck just once in all her time on the Swan, *late at night, while Chase and Keiji were asleep. Kingsford was in his usual position in the pilot's chair with his feet up on the console, staying awake late on watch, keeping one eye on the debris field the* Swan *was moving through and one eye on a grainy, buffering feed of the Cimmerian Clash, which he had $500 riding on. He looked at Nisha suspiciously as she stooped through the door.*

"What do you want?" he said.

"Just taking a look. Don't have a heart attack, old man."

"A look at what?"

Nisha sat down at the nav desk. "The map. If you have one. Where are we going after High Brazil?"

"We don't know yet," Kingsford said, turning back to his football game. "We don't have a cargo yet, and we won't until we get there. This isn't a Star Queen cruise liner."

"No shit," Nisha said.

Kingsford snorted. "Believe you me, girlie, there are worse places than this to wash up."

"Speak for yourself," she said. "Where are we likely to go after High Brazil, then?"

Kingsford sighed, rolled his chair over to the nav desk, tapped a few buttons. A three dimensional model of the solar system appeared in the hazy glow of the downlight. He tapped a few more keys, highlighting the two dozen major asteroids in the main belt, the places with a population of more than a million. Then some more – the other thousand settled asteroids, with populations anywhere between a few dozen and hundreds of thousands – and then he highlighted the routes between them, all the thousands of shipping lanes and gravity slingshots and curving flight paths. "Now let's speed it up a little," he said. "Just by a couple of weeks, fair transit time." The asteroids began noticeably moving through their orbit, some fast, some slow, some stubbornly against-the-stream retrograde, some highly inclined above the plane of the rest of the solar system. The movement of the asteroids was confusing enough, but the impact on the flight paths was worse. The shipping network had been a complicated web even from the beginning, but now it resembled a thousand brightly-coloured slinkies snarled together, tumbling in zero gravity, forever gyrating through an unpredictable tangle.

"We go where we go," Kingsford said. "And it could be anywhere." He turned the display off and rolled back over to the flight console.

Nisha left the flight deck without saying anything else. Sulky, that one, Kingsford thought. Bad luck to have a woman on a ship. Like that one he'd crewed on out of Saturn back in the '70s, what had her name been? The grouchy first mate who'd sold him out to the local cops in the Hildas after that cock-up on Asplinda. Okay, so he'd been stealing from the safe, but still.

Well out of that now, he thought. Hopeless business. Well out of that.

Chase and Keiji sat at their corner table in El Gato Negro for three hours after the lunch rush finished, and the early dinner crowd began to trickle in. "How long do you want to wait for her?" Chase said. "I mean, really. They're open till midnight. There comes a point where she's just not coming, you know?"

Keiji made a neutral noise, staring at the stained mess at the bottom of his coffee cup. He was starting to wonder the same thing. He was starting to wonder if perhaps he'd been wrong, and she wouldn't come here at all.

"What's his name?" Chase asked.

"Who?"

"The guy. The rancher. You know, the one we're delivering to."

"Techero," Keiji said. "Same as the guy on Nuevo Navarre. They're cousins. I forget his first name."

"He owns this place, too?"

"I guess."

"Uh-huh," Chase said. "You don't think he might wonder why the guy who's supposed to be delivering his fancy new cattle embryos is having a four-hour lunch at his tapas bar instead?"

"He doesn't know what I look like," Keiji said.

"Unless his cousin took a photo of you," Chase pointed out.

Keiji frowned. "We're not dealing with the Mangala Tong here. They're businessmen, not criminal masterminds."

"So why haven't you done him the courtesy of telling him we're having a little trouble with his cargo?"

Keiji threw his hands in the air. "What am I going to say? 'One of my passengers stole your cargo, but don't worry, I'm sitting in your restaurant waiting for her to try to sell it to you? And by the way, you can probably offer her much less for it, so really, it's a win-win for you?' Yeah. Great idea. Fucking brilliant."

"Hasn't he tried to get in touch with you?"

"No. We had to skirt that debris field outside Yalta, remember? I didn't know when we were getting here so I didn't set a time for the meeting."

Chase ate the last of the octopus and left his napkin scrunched up in the bowl. "Well, here's a thought. Have you tried calling Nisha?"

Keiji chuckled. "No, I'm serious," Chase said. "What do you have to lose?"

"My dignity."

"Well, we need to pack this in eventually, man," Chase said. "Cut our losses. I mean, hey, look at it this way: you got to do the right thing for your conscience or whatever back on Ganymede, she got to even it up financially so there's no hard feelings, *and* you had sex. Admit it, that's not a bad few weeks."

"Shut up," Keiji hissed, lowering his face. "Shut up shut up shut up."

"Oh my God. Is she here?"

"Don't turn around. Just... don't turn around."

The rain was still bucketing down outside, and Nisha had come down the steps wet and bedraggled, without an umbrella. She spoke to the teenager behind the bar for a moment, who nodded and disappeared out the back. She waited by the bar, idly surveying the restaurant. Keiji kept his eyes glued on the menu, an elbow on the table with a hand propping up his face to shield his features. But the restaurant was filling up again for the dinner hour, and Nisha was on the far side, and the only light was from the dozens of candles in wax-encrusted wine bottles at every table. She wouldn't see them.

"What are we waiting for?" Chase hissed. "Let's go."

"No," Keiji said. The teenager had reappeared behind the bar, and then directed Nisha down a passageway, past the toilets. "We're not doing it here."

"Why the hell not?" Chase said, leaning forward. Keiji could see his Webley holstered in his left armpit, hidden by his jacket.

"What's that going to look like? We burst into a backroom, explain to Techero's goons that she stole it from us? What do they care? They're getting it anyway. No. Let her sell it, then we go after her and take the money."

"How do you even know she's going to come back through here?"

"What do you mean?"

Chase sighed. "Well, not that you'd know anything about this, Keiji, but bars and restaurants tend to have *back doors*."

Keiji hesitated for a moment. Then he jumped to his feet, tossing a few hundred peso banknotes onto the table. "Gracias!" he called to the bemused kid behind the counter, as he and Chase scrambled up the stairs and out into the rain.

The Black Swan *was Keiji's ship, and his livelihood, but most importantly she was his home. He'd lived alone in her for years on Mars, slowly fixing her up and dreaming of the stars, and the nature of his crew was as important to him as the quality of her oxygen or the whereabouts of her next cargo. Chase he'd found bleeding out at the edge of a highway in Aaru, badly wounded from an encounter with old enemies; Keiji had taken him in, stitched him up, and they'd slowly become solid friends. Kingsford was a more recent addition, a pilot they badly needed; Keiji had rescued him from the grip of a criminal syndicate in Elysium City he'd foolishly gone into debt with. The pilot was older than Keiji and Chase combined, and something of a grumpy old coot, but he was loyal and reliable and in terms of living together they all got along fine.*

Nisha, though, made Keiji uncomfortable in his own home. Her anger over the incident back at Jupiter, her contempt for his whole operation, her constant stalking up and down the corridors like a caged tiger – all of these things wore away at his nerves. She was unhappy, and she made the crew unhappy. Yet every time they made landfall she refused to leave the Swan, *frightened of what might be waiting for her out there, after her failure – Keiji's failure, really – back on Ganymede.*

She seemed to relax somewhat after Nuevo Navarre,

on the long three-week voyage to Corduba. Keiji wasn't sure why. Maybe her anger was fading, or maybe she felt calmer as the dangers that she was convinced awaited her in the more settled worlds receded, as the Black Swan *curved further away from civilised space out into the remoter reaches of the asteroid belt. She started eating with the rest of them at dinner in the galley, watching movies on the couch in the mess, exercising on the equipment Chase had assembled in one of the unoccupied cabins.*

And then one evening, quite unexpectedly, after Chase had wandered off to bed half-drunk and Kingsford had retired to the flight deck for the evening to keep watch, she'd kissed him. And then they'd ended up in his cabin together. Keiji had been unsure of what to expect from her ever since he'd let her aboard on Ganymede, but it hadn't been that.

Keiji typically leaned towards men, but he liked women as well, and Nisha certainly fell within his parameters. It was just a shame about her personality. She may have mellowed compared to her early weeks on the Swan, *but she was still fairly prickly, and even after nights together she seemed distant. She was sleeping with him out of boredom and frustration, Keiji supposed, though why she'd chosen him over Chase he wasn't sure.*

"Why do you do this?" she asked him one night in the darkness of his cabin, lit only by the red glow of his bedside UTC clock and the distant, lonely lights of the stars.

"Uh," he said. "You came to my cabin."

She made a contemptuous noise. "I mean this. The Black Swan. *Being a ship captain. I looked you up, you know."*

"Oh." Keiji's family wasn't quite so wealthy and powerful that they were a household name, at least

outside Zutphen, but they certainly had a profile. "That's a long story, I guess."

"I don't mean, why didn't you follow in Daddy's footsteps or whatever," she said. "I mean, why this? Why running a tramp freighter?

Keiji didn't answer for a moment, listening to the dull throb of the fusion engines below the floor of his cabin. Out the porthole was a fixed, immoveable pattern of stars; only the atmosphere of a planet made them twinkle. "I guess... I guess I always wanted to travel. See things. Master of my ship. Metaphorically, I mean. Which I guess became literally." He rolled onto his side to face her. "What about you? How did you get into..." There was no nice way of saying "thief", even if it was the classy and exciting kind of thief that undertook daring art heists.

"That thing back at Jupiter was once in a lifetime, you know," she said. "I don't usually do stuff like that. I mean... that was big."

"Normally just stick to stealing from ordinary people?" Keiji said. He'd meant it as a joke, but regretted it immediately. She went cold; got dressed, left his cabin. In any normal relationship he would have called out after her, apologised, tried to fix things. But he didn't have to here, because he didn't really like her, and she didn't really like him. It was oddly satisfying, and honest. And it couldn't have left a mark, because she still came to his cabin more nights than not for the rest of the voyage to Corduba.

"I understand why you took the stupid sword back," she said one night. "I'm still pissed off at you, but I get why you did it."

"Very perspicacious of you."

"I just don't get you," she said. "Chase said that on Blomanda somebody offered you two hundred grand to ship a cargo of explosives to Callisto. Why didn't you take that?"

"I'm not a fucking war merchant," Keiji said.

"You think the rebels aren't going to get bombs any other way?" she pressed. "It's happening. You may as well take a cut."

"And end up serving a life sentence in Tulinsky with a cellmate nicknamed Vlad the Impaler?" Keiji said. "No thanks."

"Right," she said. "So, you might as well run the exact same risks by smuggling – what was it, in the end? – ninety kilos of fucking macadamia nuts into High Brazil."

"Okay, first of all, that import ban is completely ridiculous," said Keiji, suddenly heated. "Brazil nuts suck, nobody likes Brazil nuts, and they need to accept that industry's never going to take off. Okay? And secondly, somehow I don't think the consequences for contravening a customs ban are going to be quite as harsh as they are for selling bombs to an insurgency movement most governments have listed as a terrorist organisation."

"Okay," she said. "What about Nuevo Navarre?"

"What about it?"

"Chase said someone offered to sell you a load of counterfeit bioware."

"Oh, that guy. That was ridiculous. He wanted two hundred and fifty for the kind of shit you might buy in St Kaballa. I almost laughed in his face."

"So you have no issues, per se, with shipping counterfeit bioware?"

"Not really. It was our first cargo, actually. Why?"

She sat up, frustrated still, but delighted to have cracked what she perceived as a chink in his logic. "You're a hypocrite! You just pick and mix the shit you think is ethically okay. Take a look at Jupiter. Admit it! You knew that I was hiring you to pick up stolen goods. You knew you were becoming an accessory to theft. And when you found it was something you had a sentimental attachment to, you flipped out. Would you have done the same thing if I'd stolen something precious from a Muslim mosque? Or a Hindu temple? Or a Christian church?"

Keiji didn't say anything. "You wouldn't," she said. "Would you?" He could see her teeth glinting in the starlight. She was grinning.

"Good to see that every single person I manage to bring aboard this ship wants to pick holes in my decisions," he muttered.

"Funny, that," she said. "Almost as though you're the one who's wrong."

He'd hit her with a pillow, and they'd fallen to playfighting, and then had sex again before falling asleep. Between Nuevo Navarre and Corduba, Keiji thought she was definitely in a better mood. No more pacing, no more grumpiness, no more snide comments. She came to his cabin most nights, and she ate meals with the rest of the crew in the mess. He was starting to get used to having her around. He was starting to like her. He was starting to hope, from the off-hand comments she'd made, that maybe she wasn't the wealthy, high-flying kaito she'd made herself out be at the Cabaret Voltaire on Jupiter Junction; a woman with a grander network than he could dream of, friends and allies and contacts scattered in high places across the system. He was starting to think that the Black Swan was a good place for her, cruising aimlessly across the solar system with the other misfits. He was starting to hope that maybe she'd stick around. He'd been happy for a long time, ever since he'd acquired the Swan, but now he was starting to feel a second, unexpected layer of happiness swell up inside him.

He wondered later how much of it had been an act. On her part, and on his, because he'd wanted to believe it.

The sky above Cascade had turned dark grey with the coming of the storm. The core of the downpour had passed, but it was still persistently raining, the creeks and canals swollen and the streets derelict. Distant thunder crackled over the lake. Keiji wondered about that, standing beneath an awning across the street from El Gato Negro, the raindrops drumming a steady tattoo on the canvas above him. Surely thunder would upset the cattle herds, on which so much of Corduba's economy relied? He accepted that it couldn't all be sunshine and sangria, that the asteroid was a living, breathing biome which needed a hydrocycle to keep on living – or actually, did it even need that? Why couldn't they just pipe water in underground? The entire place was one big fish tank, really, a human environment built from scratch. So why did he have to be standing here with rainwater dribbling through a split in the awning and down the back of his neck?

"Any sign yet?" Chase's voice echoed in his ear. He was around the back of the bar; Keiji was across the street from the front, in case Nisha came back out the main door after all.

"No."

"I gotta say, man," Chase's voice said, *"I'm liking this. I feel pumped, you know? This is exciting. This breaks up all the interplanetary crawling a bit."*

"I'm glad my financial disasters keep you amused."

"I'm just saying. This is, all things considered, the best job I've ever had. I just want you to know that."

"You realise your payment comes as a dividend, right? A percentage of my total profit? So some of this money is *your* money. You do realise that?"

"Yeah, what is that again? Like, 2%?"

"Hey, pal, I'm the one who put in for the ship."

"Yeah, whatever. I'm not fussed. As long as there's

food on the table and the Swan *stays in the air... oh shit. She's here!"*

Chase's voice broke off in a sudden, painful exhalation. Keiji broke cover, dashed across the street through the pattering rain, threw himself down the steps that led to the alleyway behind El Gato Negro. He arrived just in time to see two figures embroiled in a struggle by the rubbish chutes. Chase was slammed up against the wall and then flipped onto the ground. A figure in a dark coat carrying an attaché case vanished down the other end of the alley.

Keiji knelt down beside his friend. "Holy *shit*," Chase wheezed, crawling onto his hands and knees. "Did not expect that. Go! I'm right behind you!"

Keiji dashed down the alley and saw Nisha ducking left onto a main road, the attaché case still in hand. "Nisha!" he shouted, but his voice was drowned in the drumming of the raindrops beating down on roof tiles and swirling through gutters. "*Nisha!*"

She glanced back but kept running, and Keiji chased after her. They emerged onto Romanos Rambla, the long boulevard now deserted in the rain. She cut in front of a tram which angrily dinged its bell, and Keiji went behind it, sloshing through the wake it left in the puddles. They were at a point where the avenue met the Grand Canal, running alongside it, and now she was headed across a bridge. Nisha slipped in a puddle, smashed her hip, and Keiji managed to close the gap a little more before she scrambled to her feet and was up and running again.

Halfway across the bridge she suddenly stopped. Keiji was too surprised to stop running, so he was only a few metres behind her when she turned around and pulled out Chase's Webley, levelling it at his face.

He stopped very suddenly. The rain was still coming down, plastering wisps of hair across her face, running in waves down her coat, dripping from the barrel of the gun. Somewhere beneath them came the doleful hooting of a barge horn.

Keiji raised his hands. "Nisha..." he said.

"Why are you chasing me?" she shouted, as thunder rumbled out over the lake. "You know you owe me! So why are you chasing me?"

"Because you ran," Keiji said.

She tilted her head, still aiming the gun at him. "Miss me, huh?"

"Seriously," he said. He was shivering, and not just from the cold of the rain. "Why did you do this? I thought..."

She shook her head, half in irritation, half in amusement. "Give Chase his gun back, would you?" she said, and threw the Webley at him.

Keiji was so surprised he fumbled the catch, the gun clattering to the pavement. Beyond that sudden engagement of hand-eye coordination, through his own clumsy hands, he glimpsed a flurry of movement: Nisha bracing one hand on the railing, the other still holding the case, pivoting her whole body up and over, vaulting down into the canal.

He rushed to the edge. There was a barge passing below, moving out of the city and onto the lake, the cargo tied down beneath taut tarpaulin. Nisha had landed safely and was waving goodbye – whether as a taunt or a genuine farewell, he couldn't say.

He watched the barge fade away into the blurry haze of rainfall, water trickling down his hair, soaking through his jacket into his shirt. A few minutes later Chase came wheezing up onto the bridge, still clutching his solar plexus. "Man, she got me *good*," he wheezed. "I just coughed up blood. She caught me by surprise, y'know? I thought I'd just talk to her, not fight her, but she really came at me fast, and..."

"Sorry, Chase," Keiji said, handing his gun back to

him. "No excuses. A girl beat you up. That's how we're remembering it."

A few hours later the *Black Swan* was on its way out of Corduba, hovering in the weightless gravity spine near the brilliant light of the faux suns, queuing behind dozens other vessels waiting to exit the Aft Gate and leave the bubble of a warm biome for the cold vacuum of outer space. With nowhere better to aim for, Keiji had set a course for San Alban, the closest large asteroid. He didn't like leaving a world without a fresh cargo, but he wanted to be well clear of Corduba.

Kingsford was sitting in the pilot's chair on the flight deck asking ATC how long the wait was going to be, Chase was somewhere down below in the mess still hurting from Nisha's beatdown, both physically and psychologically, and Keiji was sitting in the co-pilot's chair, morosely staring out the cockpit windshield at the landscape down below him. He could make out a herd of cattle the size of ants on the spinward side of the lake, slowly trudging across paddocks still soggy from the afternoon storm, wrangled by a trio of gaucho on wheeling, feisty horses. The streams and rivers of Cascade were glinting in the light of the dimming faux suns, as artificial night slowly came to Corduba.

His computer pinged. He had a message, from Nisha. He glanced over at Kingsford, who was still haranguing some poor air traffic controller for his mediocre English skills. He opened the message.

Keiji,

Sorry it went down like that. I hope I didn't hurt Chase too bad. He kind of surprised me.

I have enough to re-establish myself. Not enough to make up for what you cost me with your attack of conscience on Jupiter. Especially since that cost me more than money. But all things considered, I'm willing to say we're even now.

Hope we cross paths again one day.

Nisha x

Keiji read it again, as the ATC rep finally lost patience with Kingsford and hung up on him. "Christ!" the old man said, lighting a cigarette. "We're going to be stuck here for hours. Some fuckwits clipped the walls and depressurised their ship on the way out, so the ground crew's gotta scrape their guts out of the airlock. Made a real mess job of it, by the sound of things." He exhaled, tapped ash into an empty coffee mug, and glanced at Keiji. "Who was that message from? Don't tell me it was that bitch."

"What's your problem?' Keiji said. "She didn't do anything to you."

"Yeah, well, I was a young man once upon a time as well, you know?" Kingsford said. "Easy for your balls to choke your brain when you're making your mind up about a woman."

"Thank you for that revolting analogy."

"So was it from her, or what?"

"None of your business."

"It was, wasn't it?" Kingsford smirked.

Keiji didn't say anything for a bit. Then, in an ill-advised moment of candour, he said, "Do you think love is real?"

"Good lord," Kingsford said. "I tell you what, son, that girl did you a favour by running off. Saved you from yourself."

Keiji drummed his fingers on the console. "Remind me never to ask for romantic advice from my bitter, washed-up pilot." He stood up to mope off down the passageway, as the *Black Swan* continued slowly corkscrewing up Corduba's gravity spine towards the open freedom of space.

"Well, that was mean," Kingsford muttered.

Down in the mess, Chase was curled up in the battered green armchair, watching an old movie and smoking a joint to take the edge off the pain from the beating he'd taken. "Are we back in space yet or what?" he asked, as Keiji came down the corridor from the flight deck and flopped onto the couch.

"Not yet," Keiji said. "What are you watching?"

"Some old American romantic comedy," Chase said. "This is, like, the break-up phase before they get back together." An unbelievably pretty young man was dejectedly going through life after losing his loved one, trudging down to the supermarket in his dressing gown, buying a bottle of whiskey first thing in the morning, and challenging the clerk's facial expression with a defiant one of his own.

Keiji stared at the TV, and hazarded the question again. "Do you think love is real?"

"Oh my *God*. Don't tell me you were in love with her."

"Oh, fuck off. What would you know anyway?"

Chase passed the joint over to him. "I know enough to know that she was bad news. She used us, man. She used on Jupiter, and she used us after that."

Keiji exhaled, and passed it back. "Aren't we all using each other, though? One way or another? I mean, you guys were the ones telling me I did wrong by her back on Ganymede and it was only fair she took my cargo now. Right?"

Chase shrugged. "Just draw a line under it, I'd say. All over. Move on."

"You didn't answer my question, though. Is love real?"

Chase sighed. "Love between a man and a woman,

or love between a man and a particularly delicious strain of cannabis?"

Keiji smiled, pulled his boots off, relaxed deeper into the aged and weathered fibres of the couch. "What about love between a man and a couch?"

"Well, shit, I think that's all you can really ask for."

They passed the joint back and forth, watching a two-hundred-year-old movie, talking and laughing, ensconced in the comforting, familiar realm of the *Black Swan*'s mess as the ship patiently crawled up the queue to the Aft Gate and the familiar open roads of space. For the moment that outside world and its diverse potential was far beyond: through the rusting bulkheads stuffed with thermal insulation and rat poison, out past the radiation shielding plates, through the thick alloys of the ship's hull; through the air, the carefully controlled oxygen/nitrogen mix of Corduba's atmosphere, down, down, down through the spiralling clouds of cirrus and cumulus and nimbus, wreathed in patterns around the asteroid's golden spine of light, down past the weather drones and airplanes and gliders, down past the gaucho on the plains, the rumbling herds of cattle, the raindrops beaded on stalks of wheat, the rivers and streams and hillsides of cypress trees waving in the breeze, down through the fertile imported soil of Corduba, down through the underground hydration lines and data cables, through the maintenance tunnels to the thick, robust shell of the O'Neill cylinder, through the native outer rock of the asteroid itself, the true soil of Corduba – and then finally out and free, out into the infinite realm of space, with a thousand worlds glittering and beckoning across the great divide.

Mitchell Edgeworth's previous stories in this series were "Homecoming" (#40), "Drydock" (#42), "Flight" (#43), "Customs" (#46), "Abandon" (#47) and "Heritage" (#50). He keeps a blog at www.grubstreethack.wordpress.com.

Dodge Sidestep's (and Martin's) Final Dastardly Plan

Howard Watts

The reception desk began to lose patience with me as I held the stylus motionless in the air above the registration screen, save for a slight nervous quiver.

"Marbletech, Astrea, *Marbletech?*" I couldn't believe hearing my own words, they sounded as though my mouth was full of cotton wool – you know, the small cylindrical ones the dentist uses when you're having your wisdom teeth out.

Astrea nodded, frowning at me as she leaned upon the desk. "Yes, Marbletech. Why, is there a problem?"

"Problem?"

Yes, she could say that. I dropped the stylus and the desk sighed. "Sir, if you don't mind, there's a queue."

I glanced behind me at the holidaymakers that were looking over each other's shoulders at us. Some of them recognised us from the show, but the desk had obviously missed it for some reason – or didn't care. I looked down to my suitcase, nodding to it to follow me as I retreated. Sammy trundled behind me, still muttering I'd not colour co-ordinated properly or packed enough underpants and handkerchiefs for the trip, so I told him to be quiet. My mind reeled with Astrea's revelation, and if I didn't know better, I would have thought I'd been subjected to a dentist's injection prior to having wisdom teeth removed and my thought processes were still suffering from the drug's effect. I concentrated and my thoughts swam back over the years, to that fateful day at school. I stopped by a circular seating area near reception and sat down, Astrea sitting by my side.

"Astrea, was your mum a games mistress?"

She raised her eyebrows with surprise, "Yes, at Wolverhampton Secondary. Why do you ask, how do you know?"

I couldn't look her in the eye, pretending to watch Sammy who remained dutifully silent. "Do you have any brothers or sisters?"

"No Martin, mum never married. I'm an only child. What's this all about?"

"Bear with me. Astrea, if you don't mind me asking – how old are you?"

"I'm twenty five."

So that was it. The bloody universe had brought us together only to wave a cursory finger at me with a smarmy grin, whilst it "tut tut tutted" away at me, passing if off as background radiation or a star's wobble. Perhaps the guys at SETI had picked up the, "tut, tut, tut," repeating over and over again as I stood in that lovely Ultra Grand Hotel nestled on Eastbourne's seafront, with an ultra-lovely woman, and I wondered what the hell anything and everything was all about. I didn't have time to tell SETI they were searching for extra-terrestrial idiots with a proclivity for extracting the urine, and was wondering how to tell Astrea of my somewhat considerable concern. There was only one way, and looking back I now know there always is, as the truth has one road, and when you get to the fork, take it.

"Astrea, it seems to me there's a very high probability I'm your father."

As her mouth opened without a sound, her suitcase lay on its side and unfastened a small pocket, revealing her Gleampipe ticket home.

She placed her hands on her lap as her shoulders slumped. "How high a probability?" she sighed.

"Oh, well, it's an estimate, but probably around the 99.9 percent mark."

We turned our suitcases off lest they distracted us as Astrea's luggage launched into her, "I told you so, you can tell so much about a man from what he packs or doesn't for such a trip," routine, and I explained the whole thing.

"But why wasn't any of this mentioned in Dodge's trial?" said Astrea.

"Well, then it didn't seem important. Now..."

She shook her head and stood. "I've got to go – no, I've got to talk to mum."

I looked up to her, holding out my hands in innocence. "Astrea you must realise, I didn't know you existed until three minutes ago," realising three seconds later that was probably the worst thing I could have said.

She stopped, and for a few moments I thought she would sit back down to talk this though. "That's just part of the problem." With that she snatched up her Gleampipe ticket then picked up her suitcase, carrying it to the booth. Within moments she was gone.

I returned to the queue and finally booked a single room, then found myself walking along Eastbourne seafront, wondering what the hell could possibly go wrong next in my life, and why I'd decided to stay here. Perhaps there was a chance I wasn't Astrea's father, I tried to convince myself. I took a tour of Eastbourne's attractions in a self-driving mono-pod, and as it wheeled around the town for approximately seventeen minutes rabbiting on with great electronic gusto about the architecture and history of the place, I noticed an Equal Opportunities World Authority office. I paid the mono-pod's fee then jumped out, deciding to vent my dissatisfaction with the universe with a good old fashioned rant.

As I entered I was surprised to be greeted by an actual person sitting behind a desk. Immediately my mood improved, artificial intelligence is never very good at showing compassion, as you're no doubt already aware.

"Can I help, sir?" said the tall suited man as he stood and offered me his hand. "I'm Keith."

"I hope so, Keith," I said as I shook it with enthusiasm, "life's treated me unfairly."

He looked at me with recognition. "You were on the Ex-Con Factor last night. Martin, isn't it?"

I nodded.

He pointed a thin finger at me and began to waggle it around as he smiled behind narrowed eyes. "You managed to thwart Dodge Sidestep a second time – I read about that case a while ago." He regained his composure and sat down quickly. "But that's not why you're here, is it?" he said, handing me a glossy leaflet. His voice sharpened, honed to sales mode, and I began to realise I'd soon know if I would have been better off talking to the hotel's desk. "The EOWA *only* issues Fairness Guaranteed Certificates to newly born citizens." He clasped his hands together and placed his chin upon them. "I'm afraid you don't qualify for any addressments to your personal circumstances – not that you'd need them considering the other night's outcome." I placed the leaflet on the table before me, rotating it one hundred and eighty degrees to face him. "So, Keith, how is that fair, just because I wasn't born yesterday?"

He picked up the leaflet and placed it back into its Perspex holder, tapping it down whilst obviously stemming the almost overwhelming temptation to inform me I was behaving as though I had been born yesterday. For a few seconds I considered countering with the fact that infants cannot converse clearly at such an early juncture in their lives, and that therefore telling me such would be as inaccurate as it would be out of context, but then he spoke. "Err, it isn't fair – it's just the way the EOWA charter operates."

"I know the world's unfair, but why can't it for once be unfair in my favour? How can you purport to be representing equal opportunities when it comes to fairness? Surely your organisation is a contradiction, as it discriminates directly against me because I'm an adult."

He shrugged and leaned forward, whispering almost apologetically. "Look, I've only just taken this job – minimum wage of £78 an hour. People come in here with their children's birth certificates, I check them, log them, they pay me the £55,000 fee, I issue them with a Fairness Guaranteed Certificate for their kid – it's that simple. The FGCs are not issued retrospectively. You don't fall under our 'Protected Characteristics' list, sorry, Martin."

I let out a rasp of condescension. "That seems to be a high price for fairness. Can I speak to your supervisor?"

He rasped back in fluent bullshit as he straightened up. "By all means price it up yourself. There isn't a supervisor, such a position isn't needed – it's just me." I was about to say something when he continued. "Listen, the business has had all kinds of rubbish thrust upon it since opening. We've had various England world cup squads complaining that being beaten on penalties eight tournaments in a row isn't fair, people moaning that it rained on their birthdays, that the person they married didn't live up to their expectations, that coincidence doesn't always lead to serendipity and that the universe is somehow against them."

"A-ha!" I said, "that's why I'm here."

He looked confused. "You're not part of the next England world cup squad, are you?"

"Certainly not, I..."

"So, it rained on your birthday?"

"No," I said, "that's just bad luck."

He explained there wasn't a department for bad luck, so I went on to clarify my real reason for talking to him, that meeting a woman who has similar feelings towards me as I do to her, who turns out to be my daughter, simply wasn't fair.

He nodded, almost with recognition which was disconcerting. I leaned forward in my seat and smiled, hoping for a favourable reply that could somehow correct this mess.

"Does she have any sisters? You know, of a different father – perhaps you could meet one of them." He seemed genuinely excited and enthusiastic by his own stupidity. "You know, same upbringing, location. They might be similar in looks, tastes and – well, you know?"

Keith was trying to help, I'll give him that. But I pressed on; convinced I had a good case.

We debated back and forth until lunchtime – and decided both of us had been served a raw deal and that we'd just have to get on with it – the poor guy told me he was on a zero seconds contract that could be cancelled anytime, and had a wife and several kids living in a tiny principality of what used to be called Russia, and that the majority of his earnings was automatically transferred to them, forcing him to live on a *Meal in a Mug*™, four days a week. I wished him luck, adding the beef stroganoff flavour was the most authentic. He thanked me for this and gave me his business card – adding that perhaps one day I'd have a child and that I should talk to him. I walked out into the sunshine deciding to head for the nearest pub, deceiving myself that a pint and a pie would make my whole life seem so much better in comparison to his.

As I sat at the bar I turned on my phone to see if Astrea had messaged me again. She hadn't, so I began chatting with the little device as it seemed to me to be my only friend. It complained that I only ever used it to check the weather, and that that was getting a little depressing. I quickly explained that if it could ever get over the argument it had had well over a year ago with the location service application, it would realise we lived in the UK. It vibrated with a shrug then moaned about being kept in the dark over all this, and I explained my pocket was the best place for it. It didn't like my humour, then surprisingly said something profound.

"There's only one person that can help you."

"Is there, do I know him or her?"

"Of course. If anyone can figure out how to right all this mess, it's Dodge Sidestep. Together you'd come up with a plan."

I couldn't argue with my phone on this occasion – despite all the false Google leads it had fed me regarding the correct way to fold an omelette – as it had in this case a very valid point. Dodge was a schemer, he had an uncanny ability to traverse every aspect that life thrust upon him that he didn't agree with – hence his nickname. Something in his past had caused him to act this way, to develop his ability to dodge life's unfairness and slap life back in the face. I thought about it and realised there *had* to be a way to hack into his loop, to join him in his infinite journey towards his inevitable death and somehow rescue him. I had to trust him – he'd see the unfairness of the whole situation and help me. He was, as my phone had said, the only person that could help, and at one time (albeit a long time ago) a friend.

I gleamed over to his address. His living room was lit by the late afternoon sun which struggled uneasily through the partially open blinds. Still crammed with appliances the room was cold and unwelcoming, as I remembered the last time I stood there. I powered up his answering appliance and waited. Finally the image of the old Dodge appeared before me.

"Hello Martin. I didn't think I'd see you again. Did you have your hair cut?"

"I did. Dodge, listen, I've got myself, and your real self, in a spot of bother. Care to help?"

The image nodded and gave me a grin. As I relayed the whole sorry episode Dodge shook his head with the sheer complexity and strangeness of the whole affair. "A closed Gleampipe loop's not easy to find, without a reference point it's practically impossible," he said as he paced up and down. "Even if you do find it, cutting in is problematic at best."

"I'm aware of that – hence asking you. Where would *you* situate such a loop, if it – well, it is, was you, that devised it?"

He thought about it for a while, walking around the room and admiring his future self's collection of appliances. Finally he turned to me. "He wanted you to be trapped in the loop, that much we know. He'd certainly want to gloat, and watch your despair and ultimate death." He powered up the music system and it hummed, so Dodge told it to be quiet. I turned up the lights and joined him as he began running a system check on every component.

"His personal booth has recent information in the buffer, look."

I squinted at the screen. There was a group of four numbers repeating over and over again, scrolling up the screen. 00110001 00110110 00110001 00111000.

"Binary," I said.

"Yes," said the old Dodge, "but what does it mean, I've not learnt binary?"

I thought about it, then realised. "It's 1618 in text, does that mean anything to you?"

"Fibonacci's!" he said.

"This is no time for ordering a pizza," I answered, "and if it's with mushrooms, which it sounds like it is – I hate mushrooms, they just look evil."

He ignored my mycophobia. "No, Fibonacci's math sequence, you got the Italian reference right at least. He was a mathematician from the middle ages and his sequence explains a spiral. Perhaps Dodge is in a spiral and not a loop, as the binary means 1.618, Fibonacci's golden number."

I thought hard for a while then it hit me. "If you translate the binary to octal, it comes out at 6115430470." We looked at each other and spoke simultaneously. "The dialling address for this booth."

"He's running a spiral journey, never ending, looping back on itself like a crazy helter skelter that only Esher could draw," I declared as I dialled in the booth's own address and stepped in before Dodge could say another word or convince me otherwise.

It was the first time I'd ever felt pain during a Gleampipe journey, save for the time I actually used one to visit the dentist to have my wisdom teeth extracted. But this pain was totally different. It was as though I was being squashed rather than stretched, as though I'd decided to take a holiday on the surface of Jupiter. My cells screamed at me one by one, and just when I thought I'd made the wrong decision, the pain vanished.

I found myself standing on an old school bus from my youth. Outside the scenery raced by at incredible speed, the vehicle refusing to stop at bus stops where groups of children dressed in school uniforms waited, their shouts dissipating as the imaginary vehicle sped by their imaginary faces. As I looked ahead and behind I could see the bus appeared to be infinite, thousands of seats without a single passenger. Some way off ahead of me were the stairs to the top deck, so I ran to them. As I reached the bottom step I could hear someone whistling. The tune was unmistakeable; it was the chorus to the Beatles' "Helter Skelter". I trod the steps quietly and upon reaching the upper deck I could see a figure way off in the distance sitting at the front of the bus. I ran towards them. It seemed to take an age to reach them, and when I did I slumped down into the seat opposite, virtually exhausted. Dodge's whistling stopped. He spoke without looking over to me, his eyes fixed at the blurred gradients of grey fakeness ahead.

"I wondered how long it would take you to figure it out. No doubt you didn't do so by yourself?"

"No, your answering appliance helped me."

"Again? I must have words with myself about that. Still, I'm pleased to see you, Martin. You do realise I didn't plan to keep you locked away on this virtual bus until your mind and body died."

"You didn't?"

He finally turned to face me. "Of course not, it's a clue pointing to the origin of my hatred for you. My plan was to return home and recall you from this spiral journey into my home booth, and carry out my original plan," he smiled, "with a few amendments to ensure success, of course."

I was confused, no, I simply didn't understand. "Why the bus, Dodge, why this and not some other form of temporary prison?"

He closed his eyes for a moment, heaving out a long sigh of disappointment. "You didn't realise back then,

then you didn't realise when you explained it to me, and you're not able to realise it now, are you?"

I shook my head.

"You achieved something school friends always seem to be able to do, without knowing or trying, without malice or intent perhaps, but always with great heartache and emotional damage to their friends. Damage that lasts a bloody lifetime, in this case."

"What *are* you talking about?"

"Remember Miss Marbletech, the games mistress. *You* did and *I* didn't. I knew it back then as I saw you, watched you through the gym office keyhole. You finally admitted it, as if it were some great revelation to be proud of, when I had you tied up in my basement. It wasn't a revelation; it was a revulsion for me. I *loved* her and I'm sure you knew it back then, and did what you did just because you could, in spite of me." His gaze returned to the view ahead, his voice softening. "I still love her, even now, but you took her from me, ruined my hopes with a brief loveless impulse when we were kids at school." He turned and glared, raising his voice, slapping the seat beside him sending up a cloud of virtual dust. "I'll never forgive you for that, and that's why I've tried to kill you twice."

I looked away, unable to maintain his gaze, nodding finally with recognition – it all made sense now. The universe was at last giving up its secrets and I was happy with the payoff. "Dodge, about that. I think we can sort all this out together, once and for all."

He laughed and shook his head with dismissal. "And how do you come to that conclusion, old friend?" He fanned out his arms and pointed ahead. "How do you expect to stop this unending spiral journey that has us both trapped until death, how do you honestly think you can make everything right between us?"

I leant over to him and grinned. "If you've

programmed this bus correctly, then it's simple." I stood and pressed the bell four times, the emergency stop signal for the driver. Instantly the bus halted, and both Dodge and I were flung through the front windows. Glass splintered and cascaded around us as we were flung headfirst above the infinite spiral road. I watched as each tumbling shard contained images from our past, memory fragments built into this prison of hatred and regret. Virtual children at bus stops watched and pointed to us as we flew over their heads, and as we both came within an inch of the roadway our bodies were returned to Dodge's booth.

"Good," said Dodge's answering appliance as we stepped out. "I'm glad you figured out the exit subroutine trigger."

"You can't, what's happened has happened – it's simply not possible. The universe won't allow it, it's unfair," said Dodge, handing me a glass of water. I placed it on the kitchen table without taking a sip as his other self nodded in recognition with his arms folded.

"Anything's possible," I said quickly. "Look at what you've achieved with your appliances – the Strollperson™, managing to build your own from salvaged and cloned parts. Imagine what you could do with a spiral loop and enough power, using as you did the universe's golden ratio of 1.618."

I could see he was intrigued, as was his former self who took a seat at the table as Dodge spoke. "What do you have in mind?"

"Simple. Time travel."

They looked at each other. "Simple! You're calling time travel simple?" they said in unison.

"No, what I have in mind is simple, to answer your question. But thinking about it, for you, yes perhaps it is. If you don't mind me saying so we both know there's a fine line between insanity and genius – your music's been hailed as genius, and you've also been declared insane. All you have to do is apply yourself to this. Send me back in time to school, I can stop myself from sleeping with Miss Marbletech, Astrea won't be my daughter and you can, for want of a better term, fill in for me."

They both smiled and the former Dodge spoke for them both. "History will be re-written. He'll not try to kill you, everything will change, and then..."

Dodge interrupted himself. "But, Astrea, if she's even called that, perhaps won't be the person she is. You can't be one hundred percent certain you're her father, anyway – and I'm not sure I want to be."

"Anything's better than this reality, for both, sorry, all of us – wouldn't you both agree? No murder attempt, no incarceration, no more Friday night punk rock singalongs."

"Agreed," said Dodge finally.

I stood. "I'll see if I can raise some funds with Kickstarter, and you can use your prize money from winning the Ex-Con Factor."

"If this works, it really has the potential to fubar the entire world, Martin," said Dodge.

"Not if we localize the effect, clip the butterfly's wings so to speak – keep the spiral loop centralised on just you," suggested the other Dodge.

I shrugged. "Please?"

"I'll get to work," they said.

I sent Astrea a text explaining our plan, and she replied that I was insane. I should have expected that, really. But I must admit to hoping for a little assistance. I asked her to tell me about her mother, her likes and dislikes, just to give me the edge, and pass it onto young Dodge should I end up back in time at

Wolverhampton Secondary. She ignored me and blocked any further communication, saying the last person she'd ever want as a father would be Dodge Sidestep, and she didn't exactly relish the idea of waking up a totally different person. I told her there were millions of people that wish exactly that, every day of the week, and (I'll admit, without thinking) that it will be the ultimate make over. She swore at me with words that she'd obviously heard during her tenure in the Virtual Prison service, words that I refuse to repeat here for the sake of decency and envisioned anatomical impossibilities.

Dodge worked with his answering appliance, two heads being better than one and all that. They argued a little, but slowly both Dodges seemed to be happy with their agreed theory at least.

The Kickstarter funding brought in roughly twenty million quid, which was a great relief, as Dodge had decided he wanted to rent the great super collider at Cern for a couple of hours, their fee quoted at twenty million quid. There were a few opponents to our plan, of most notoriety the government's suddenly established Temporal Complaints Committee, but they soon folded as someone suggested that perhaps I'd already gone back in time thus creating this reality, and they couldn't disprove this without sending their own representative back in time to monitor my arrival, thus breaking their own rules and mucking this reality up even more. That, and (more importantly for them) if I was stopped from taking the trip they'd never need to exist in the first place to object, and neither would their quite considerable pensions and severance payments following their department's closure. It all got a bit heated, but at the end a few of those guys walked away from the whole thing with a shed load of cash for doing absolutely nothing other than having a moan and knowing someone from a government department that desperately needed to spend public cash so the same amount was allocated the following year.

Dodge's plan consisted of piggybacking a super collider particle stream with a synaptic portion of my compressed consciousness as it was extracted for travel by the Gleampipe system. Everyone that agreed this was a superb idea was quoted in various media streams, and Dodge received a Nobel Prize for the plan before it was executed. This upset quite a few people; mostly the ones that didn't realise that objecting in various media steams would afford them an equally quotable quote, but more so the ones that lied that they were working on a similar idea whilst masquerading their research as to the frequency of mental illness in tapeworms lest someone found out what they were really up to.

Then the accusations began to fly about that Dodge had travelled in time before with stolen technology. He argued that most of the time travel ideas he (and most people for that matter) had read about in the past involved wormholes, the warping and bending of space-time, time machines of various incongruous designs, travelling faster than light and stolen, borrowed or on loan alien technology. As none of these had ever been either physically proven or found, his argument held up, closing with if anyone really wanted to debate the subject and prove him wrong with their evidence, they should meet him last Tuesday. Even my phone vibrated in agreement; finally, intelligence wasn't so artificial after all. Dodge had booked a hall for the proposed debate and employed a catering service to provide sandwiches, various savoury finger foods, including prawn vol-au-vents for some reason, soft drinks and vanilla cupcakes which all went to waste. It's true, he showed the hall to me, as he knew that would be his argument all along, as he remembered no one turned up last Tuesday, including himself. Sidestep by name, sidestep by nature.

Everything seemed to be going really well, then came the court injunction from Astrea.

We represented ourselves at the hearing, Astrea represented in her absence by a small team of lawyers and physicists. A high court judge was appointed just before he was due to leave for his holiday, and the poor chap didn't seem at all happy at the prospect of presiding over the whole affair.

The crux of Astrea's opposition was murder – or rather our proposed murder of her "normal self" via time travel. We argued that this was simply not the case and that all three of us were simply trying to "Do what's right," and the fact that she actually wouldn't be dead following the plan's success. Her lawyers also went on to argue that if we did alter the past, that a new reality would suddenly leap into existence and sort of muck a lot of stuff up for a lot of people, or as they put it, *"Present severe, unpredictable outcomes posing a clear and present danger to the entire universe and the entire population's perceived reality."*

Our defence was really quite sharp, and Dodge declared that the universe simply didn't contain enough energy and matter to create a new alternate reality, that, and that *"the entire population's perceived reality"* was not only a collective term, which was a shoddy presumption as no evidence had been presented to back up this claim from the entire population, but that even seen as a singular proposition it was clearly relative, as every single human being and AI on the planet undoubtedly saw reality differently – just ask anyone – perceived *realities*. I nodded, thinking this was a reasonable argument, adding with a broad smile that, "You can't make an omelette from scrambled eggs." Astrea's team ignored my comment and thought about Dodge's, then decided to ask somebody, but nobody was interested in participating as they were all unwilling to compare realities with someone else lest someone else's was far more appealing than their own. Everybody admitted they didn't have a clue nor had absolutely any intention of learning to play second fiddle whilst they stared at the greener grass over their garden fences.

"In the scientific community," began one of Astrea's physicists, "it is a solid belief that quantum fluctuations in our universe can lead to the birth of baby universes – alternate realities."

"How do you know this reality is not a result of such a fluctuation from another universe?" countered Dodge.

"We don't."

"Can you prove this reality is not the result of either one or multiple instances of time travel conducted in our future?"

"We cannot," said another physicist, standing as the former looked down to his notes.

"So how can you possibly argue without a solid benchmark of proof this reality is the one true reality, and should be maintained at all costs – would it not be fair to argue our plan could bring about the one true reality?"

They huddled together for a minute or so, a few raised voices and sounds of "Shhh!" There was a lot of hand waving before the lead scientist addressed the judge.

"We're not absolutely sure."

I saw my opportunity as the judge called a recess and presented everybody via a press conference with the address of the Equal Opportunities World Authority office in Eastbourne, quoting the opposition's statement of, *"In the scientific community it is a solid belief that quantum fluctuations in our universe can lead to the birth of baby universes – alternate realities."*

If a baby universe/alternate reality is created, then surely the EOWO charter should give everyone a Fairness Guaranteed Certificate in that "baby" reality, as they are new born.

Both Dodges thought this was a good point to start, and poor Keith didn't know what hit him. In a matter of hours the majority of the UK's population had convinced the EOWO that our plan was essential, as nobody was content, life was unfair and demanded a reboot. *"Give us fairness now, not then!"* they cried. The EOWO offices were surrounded, the population pointing out that if this world authority couldn't address their demands, then Dodge and I must be allowed to continue with our final plan. If our plan did create an alternate reality, then everybody was willing to take the chance that this new reality would be far better than the current one and the unfairness rife in It.

"It is quite possible that if a reboot does take place, then the EOWO may perhaps be in a position to issue FGCs to everyone," said an EOWO representative, realising the revenue from such an endeavour probably wouldn't outweigh the logistical and moreover the financial problems of addressing each and everybody's concerns arising from it.

As I predicted, it all became a bit political then. The governments and various national parliaments decided they were the only ones qualified to vote on such a monumentous decision, but they soon backed down following various global outbreaks of unrest, and agreed to give the vote to the entire world. The people would have their say. Studies and predictions were made – the media streams were choked with opinions and experts' possible outcome scenarios.

Then Astrea's lead lawyer addressed the hearing the following week.

"Providing a vote for every single person on the planet is impossible, and therefore the result will not be an accurate count and invalid."

I'd never seen Dodge smile so widely at that one. "Bring in that Keith guy you met."

Keith was more than happy to help our cause, unsurprising considering his diet, and under Dodge's instruction contacted Synapse Noggin. The company was pleased with the proposition, and began manufacture of a small hand held device similar to a mobile phone. They acquired sponsorship from various companies, whose products and services scrolled across the device's little screen. Beneath the screen in raised bold red letters it read, "WOULD YOU BE HAPPY IF YOUR LIFE COMPLETELY CHANGED OVERNIGHT?" and beneath this were three buttons, "Yes", "No", and "Don't Care". These Votepads™ shipped to everyone that didn't have a connection to the voting website or a local voting station and of course to the inhabitants of the less developed regions of the world. Synapse Noggin's share price, along with their sponsors, went ballistic, making the top three net worth companies in the world Synapse Noggin, Twinkly Toes Foot Spas, and a coffee shop chain.

I did point out that if a new reality was conjured up from our plan, there was no guarantee this new reality would maintain these share prices, but Dodge told me to shut up. I did, taking peace of mind from the thought that perhaps, in this type II reality, I might get my cat back and in later life foot spas would be a damn sight cheaper.

The judge sighed, then spent a lot of time performing judicial poses as he listened to both arguments sum up. You know, leaning forwards and clasping his hands together upon his desk, raising his eyebrows, lowering his head and peering over the rim of his glasses, leaning back in his chair and removing them before closing his eyes and pinching the bridge of his nose. It all seemed a little too much for him as he finally spoke. "The people of the world will decide with a vote, thankfully this is all out of my hands."

As we walked from the court, pushing through the media frenzy waiting for us outside, I asked Dodge how he intended to project my mind into my body at the right time and place, but he just mumbled something about the universe taking care of it for him as he smiled at the cameras, and that if he had the choice he'd travel into the future then return so he could inform the UK's population when the DFS sale would actually end, and receive the Sveriges Riksbank Prize in Economic Sciences. I wasn't very happy with this explanation, as I'd enjoyed DFS's continued marketing campaign over the past several decades, enticing me to take out a 0% finance deal over the rest of my life on a corner suite that would in no way complement my lounge, but looked nice in the ridiculously large set the advertisements were filmed in. I thought about this a little more, and considered contacting them. As the world's first time traveller I could perhaps pay off the finance deal before I'd even signed it, but realised the corner suite still wouldn't fit into my flat and the whole idea was pointless, save for buying a scotch guarded footstool – again pointless, as I didn't have a cat. I used to, but it ran away with its ears trembling some time ago. I pressed on, and finally Dodge came up with another unsuitable answer that was somehow more believable than the first as we got into a cab. We could have gleamed home, but Dodge wanted to see a picture in tomorrow's papers of his self, waving from behind the cab's window as it pulled away.

"It's simple, really," he began, unconvincingly. "We know where you were living at a certain date in time and project your consciousness into your younger self via the Gleampipe protocol, when you're lying in bed asleep. It's all about coordinates and working backward, taking into account the rotation of the Earth and nailing it all down to one place in time and space. The accelerator will take care of the rest, and deliver your consciousness into your head when you were younger."

I was a little upset over this, but Dodge informed me that there was a one in six hundred and eighteen chance of success, convincing me the odds were in my favour and it would be alright and that I would be delivered to the right place at the right time. That reminded me very much of what I'd been told on the phone when I'd booked a delivery for a new dishwasher, so I was happy, as this was without a doubt a universal constant everyone had dealt with during their lives. Dodge confirmed this, telling me the delivery window for my consciousness would be roughly between the hours of 12 and 6, and that providing me with a definite delivery time was impossible.

The results of the vote came in a week later and were unsurprising really. Out of the 9,997,398,000 souls, only 130.2 million decided it was a bad idea, while 21.2 million didn't care. Statistically it was pointed out that the "No" vote number roughly equated to the number of millionaire households in the world, averaging four persons per household. A few millionaires came forward to point out they had voted "Yes", and that when you have that much money, everything kinda gets a little boring and any change is a welcomed one, but there was no proof votes were cast from any particular bracketed group or those from a recognised social position. Clearly, the world didn't mind a change or a surprise.

The day finally came and I stood outside a Gleampipe booth, situated next to and linked into the Super Proton Synchrotron.

"One thing I've not asked," I asked, as Dodge fiddled with the booth's system protocols. "How am I going to get back?"

He stopped and turned. "Get back? Back to where exactly?"

"Here, where else do you think I want to get back to – the point of departure, obviously!"

"I don't see the point," said Dodge returning to his work. "Don't forget, it's not your body that's travelling, just your mind. You'll end up in your younger self's head and take it from there, sharing the space."

"Is there enough room in my head for two consciousnesses?"

He glanced at me, briefly.

"So, what, I've got to live through all those exams and all that other crap again, growing up?"

"Yeah. All for the greater good. For both of us, remember – but don't give yourself a better grading in English lit, remember, you're rubbish?"

"If I'd remembered, I'd already have done it," I said, a little agitated, realising I hadn't as I still couldn't remember the opening line of Shakespeare's *Coriolanus*.

"Before we proceed any further, hear me speak," said Dodge. "Once you stop yourself from doing the deed and help me to, you can sit back and enjoy the ride. You can sleep inside your own head, then reawaken as you catch up to the point where everything has changed for us." He held my arm and spoke quietly. "I put a clue into my recordings – a little…"

"I know," I said quickly, "A phrase to explain your intended actions – a bunch of lyrics hidden in your covers of various tracks."

He nodded enthusiastically, "Yes, that's it. I'll do the same to wake you up. Having been dormant you'll not interfere with the way things should be, after you've substituted me to Miss Marbletech. Understand?"

I thought about it and nodded, lying. "Okay. What's the phrase?"

We discussed this for a while and came to a sensible conclusion, and a date for the delivery of the phrase, something we both remembered had happened.

"Are you ready?" said Dodge.

I nodded, then stepped into the booth.

I awoke in bed. I could hear my mother shouting that breakfast was ready, so I'd obviously been delivered at the wrong time. I found myself getting up, washing, dressing and heading downstairs. It was all very strange watching from behind my eyes as I went about my day. Later, I was on the bus to school and quickly checked my timetable. It was PE first thing, and by the look of the weather, winter. My mind sat back as my younger self went about his mundane daily tasks which consisted for the most part of being ignored by the girls, not having a ball passed to me during football, trying to be invisible during English Lit and failing whilst writing "I dislike English" in binary on the cover of my workbook, hating school lunch and then, finally, the moment came. My maths tutor asked me to deliver a note to Miss Marbletech after school. I remembered this, giving myself that déjà vu feeling so rife when you're young, so I forced myself to meet up with Dodge and bet him he didn't have the guts to deliver the note for me. From a safe distance I watched as he knocked on the gym office door. Miss

Marbletech was far more unattractive than I remembered, and I remember remembering I'd forgotten exactly how she looked, in favour of a far more attractive woman hidden in the memory inside my head – probably for the sake of fake self-esteem. Smiling at Dodge she asked him in. He kept his headphones on as the door closed and locked behind him. As quickly and as silently as I could I hurried to the door and peered through the keyhole. The deed was indeed soon done, and I hurried to the bus stop as my memory of her vanished.

When I arrived home I complained of a headache – my mother wondering if it was a reaction to having my wisdom teeth out a couple of days ago, telling me I should have an early night. As I lay there in bed I began to wonder about this entire scenario, and the recurring theme of teeth. If Dodge wasn't going to try and kill me in this timeline, then I wouldn't be able to thwart his plan, he wouldn't be convicted and I wouldn't meet Astrea – if she even ended up with that name. Panic coursed through me – all this, so simple a task upon reflection, to have to live out another sixteen years essentially hiding in my own head, there just for the ride, watching, grimacing at so many wrong decisions, so much crap. Could I just sit back and watch it all over again? My grandparents' deaths, the unfolding of what was, or rather is, history – without taking action, to right what I considered unfairness as it ran rife around me during world events, the taking of innocent lives, the ruining of my mother's attempts at soufflés? All those new films and TV shows (those god awful Saturday nights watching umpteen episodes of *Britain's Mostly Untalented*) which were for me to be repeats – how could I keep quiet? I really had no choice in the matter, and decided to sleep as my head pounded with pain. I slept for a long, long time until a familiar voice awakened me.

"Hello."

"Martin, is that you?"

"Speaking, who's that?"

"It's Dodge Sidestep. Remember me?"

"Sidestep? Oh – yeah, Dodge, of course. How's it going?"

There was a long pause and I heard music in the background, a jumbled nebulous mess. It sounded like there were three songs playing simultaneously. My head began to ache.

"It's about the money, Martin."

"Money," I said, "what money, what's that noise in the background?"

"The money I'm going to win from you. Sorry, all three of us are playing our own music at once – hold on. Mart, you still enjoy a bet, yes?" One song emerged from the cacophony, the Beatles' "Helter Skelter".

"Bet? Yes, I still enjoy a wager," I said with a suspicious frown, "from time to time, that is."

"All the time, if I know my old friend," said Dodge. "Listen, I'll wager you the cost of my latest musical appliance I've had the greatest musical experience of either of us – it's only 20k – can you cover that?"

I grinned "Don't tell me, you've got a Strollperson™ on pre order? Go on."

"I have. Anyway, remember Miss Marbletech, the games mistress?"

"Kind of." My headache transformed, like a burning sensation, my thoughts jumbled, just like the music I had heard from Dodge's. Memories began to fade, like those of a dream and the way that they sometimes surface throughout the day in tiny snippets, only to vanish at day's end. Were they reminders perhaps, incomplete slices of alternate realities, visited during slumber as the mind wanders aimlessly on its own throughout the multiverse before returning to the familiar comfort of home?

"You didn't?"

"I did and still am – well, not right now. We're married, Mart. Perhaps I can come over and collect on that bet sometime, seeing as I'm guessing you can't beat my revelation?"

My headache began to fade, but I still felt muddy, as though my thoughts were not my own, and something told me to not even bother trying to beat his experience. "Sure, Dodge, you win. It would be great to catch up. It's been a long time. Saturday okay?"

"Fine – we'll be over around 7.30, and we'll bring over Astrea, our daughter, if that's okay?"

"Sure," I said, as questions appeared in my head from nowhere, forcing themselves forward. "Just out of curiosity, what does your daughter look like, what does she do? I kind of have this mental image of her, for some strange reason."

"Oh she's blonde like her mother – straight hair. She's just been given a promotion at the Virtual Prison service, we're very proud. One thing, she's actually my stepdaughter, but I legally adopted her a long time ago as I can't have kids, so don't mention either please. She's heard a lot about you over the years and is dying to meet you in person."

I sighed inside, and my mind suddenly became blank, as though there was something so vitally important I needed to remember that had been physically taken from it. I shook the feeling off and concentrated, feeling like myself once again. "I look forward to meeting her too," I eventually said. "See you Saturday, Dodge old friend, it's been a long, long time."

Howard Watts is a writer, artist and composer living in Seaford who also provides the cover art for this issue. His artwork can be seen in its native resolution on his deviantart page: http://hswatts.deviantart.com. His novel The Master of Clouds is now available on Kindle.

Rathfern's Menagerie

Allen Ashley

Even at this late stage, there's something of a frisson about being inside a female body.

Technically, of course, this is an android body; to use the old vernacular, "a mechanical creation", one with female physical characteristics. There is enough left of my male-born consciousness to still thrill me that I am temporarily in possession of an opposite gender.

Rathfern was the brains behind all this. It's not too bold or extreme a statement to say that his genius has revolutionised modern science. He has made so many fresh choices – human or animal – open to our experience, if we're brave enough to shuck off our old physical selves and be transposed into these almost fully convincing facsimiles. Or if we have to...

As one would expect, there's always a risk associated with any such endeavour. Most times the wealth of new sensations and knowledge negates such concerns. I have known what it is like to have voluptuous breasts, delicate toes, wide hips and to... be on the receiving end. That my lover Fleur became my male partner for such a union was the clincher. I love her so much. We have explored our passions from several angles and our bond has been thus deepened.

As things stand right now, there is not much else to do aside from explore these passions. If only Rathfern were still truly with us he would know what to do, he would have ideas to take us beyond this experimentation.

A great philosopher once said, "Your future is very much like your present, only more so." This is the pattern for how things will continue. While we have a seemingly unlimited supply of nutrients to sustain us, while there are possibilities unexplored, while we can...

I am aware that essentially we are drifting through our existence. This is not the brave new world I envisaged when I said goodbye to my parents at age seven and began the thrilling ride through my advanced education and apprenticeship. But if everything was so predictable there would be no evolutionary or technological imperatives.

"That's how things are now, John," Fleur mutters from one of the preparation desks.

Today she is inside the less muscled, smoother bodied male android. She told me once that she preferred this version because it was not such a jump. I answered, "It's always a jump, darling. Our consciousnesses are part-preserved in Hi-Den-Silica and we transfer that into body shaped machines; how is that anything but a jump?"

She strokes my long hair. It's blonde, silky, artificial but indistinguishable from "real" human hair to even the most probing touch. Her dark eyes hold fondness but not passion, not this time.

"Whilst we've got the use of hands," she states, "let's run some checks on the sensors and readers."

I want to respond that we did the very same work yesterday but I bite back this errant tongue. It's something to do. It passes the time.

The procedure has robbed us of the capacity to dream, which partly explains why Fleur and I feel the need to fill our days with transference and the occupation of different bodies. The lack of a permanent home body must also be considered a factor.

We have a menagerie of android animals to entertain us and, if we are brave or foolish enough, to use as receptacles for our minds. The process is much the same as the transfer to the human shells but is fraught with more difficulty for some inexplicable reason. Inexplicable? Rathfern could have told us why, could perhaps have solved the problem given time. I believe it is due to the autonomous circuits that enable these creatures to function and behave in as close to a natural manner as possible without the incursion of our higher consciousnesses. It's most likely that invasion which causes the compatibility and stasis issues. Humankind messing about with evolution yet again.

The panda droid sits and feigns eating motions for most of the day. Each creation has a tiny sub-nuclear power source and no need to eat in the usual sense. The cat will lick at a bowl of nutrients but not ingest any. The white hand-size pet that I call "Professor Rat" doesn't even pretend to gnaw and munch at anything semi-edible. Tame animals all around us, an indoor Garden of Eden.

What nutrients we carry are to preserve the organic tissue that once housed our minds / consciousnesses / souls – you choose the description. As for our actual bodies, they are decomposed, acid burnt. Preserved frozen but uninhabitable. Rathfern and his cutting edge technology gave us this dubious freedom. Sometimes I wonder if I left the most crucial elements of myself back in that husk when I took Rathfern's offer of somewhat ambiguous, continued existence.

Whatever else the day brings, Fleur and I have a routine that we stick to. It is time to check all the readings. I say to myself that they will be the same as yesterday and the day before. The atmosphere outside will show as toxically polluted, rendered unbreathable. I check the meters and sensors. I am proven correct in my assumptions.

"Same shit out there, different day," Fleur comments. I can see both beauty and boredom behind the synth-flesh eyes of her chosen android – female today, physically perfect in the sight of some cultures.

It's the Garden of Eden and this time there is no leaving to be done.

We had a whole contingent of survivors not so long ago. One by one they have passed. I wish we could have saved them. The last to go was Davidson: the final fully flesh body. I never felt jealous of him for that and he was an able lab technician always willing to complete the transfer for Fleur or for me. Poor old Davidson. Lacking Rathfern's skills, we couldn't preserve his consciousness after the accident. Poor old us. To effect the crossover, we need hands – fingers, digits. This means that at all times one of us must be contained within a humanoid shell. Now a duo, our options for experimentation have been limited. I know my adventurous partner feels this lack even more than I do.

It's like a drug. You make the transference once and it's like being reborn. In many respects, that's the best way to describe it, a sort of scientific adaptation of Buddhist philosophies of continual rebirth. I must try harder, work my way back up the ladder of significance towards eventual nirvana.

It begins with a tingle, a sort of brain itch. Flashes of light, disembodied aural impressions, a loosening of assumed ties to the physical plane, a rising like a gentle cloud, a spreading out like a warm wave. Then the gap. Always the gap. That infinitesimal yet almost infinite moment of being nowhere. Maybe that's the truth – within that moment one is truly Nowhere.

Once lodged inside the host body, matters return to something approaching normality and it becomes a matter of establishing muscle control and sending the correct electrical impulses to one's new torso, limbs and muscles to move them around freely.

I am beginning to tire of the regular switches and wish that I could settle into one of the shells and call it my own for the duration. Fleur, though, insists on skipping from one container to another. Maybe she'll calm soon.

There was a time before all this when I had a regular job, a wife who was not Fleur, a government permit to father children after the next promotion... all gone now, that world of steady employment, economics, governance. Now the only rule is survival. If that leads us to break the old chains, so be it. My old self would have found Fleur too flighty, too prone to risk-taking. Now she is the shining beacon that lights up these dull days of the post-apocalypse.

"I'll be your kitten," she states, begging me to transfer her to another of Rathfern's mechanical menagerie. "You can stroke me all day," she adds. She's purring already as if the crossover has already happened.

I want to tell her that I would like us now to settle, perhaps once and for all, on the best of the human droids. She had short spiky hair, wiry limbs, and an elfin face when first I knew her but my mind could easily accept her in the guise of the blonde neo-goddess that Rathfern created in his workshop, would she but remain within that. Likewise, there is a male shell that is developed enough yet ordinary enough for me to feel that I could slot in and stay put for the rest of my existence. A time of change should be followed by a time of stasis.

There is still no word from the outside world. How long can we live here as disembodied souls squatting inside these astonishingly lifelike but still android frames? We seem to be truly the last remnants of Humankind. What a burden! Not something I would have wished even on my worst enemy.

The Enemy has done this. But it's rebounded back on them and hit them just as hard. Rathfern would have said something like, "The only true enemy is the one within ourselves" and he would have been correct.

If only I could bring him back. He would be like Merlin, Gandalf... Jesus... and solve all our problems.

Yesterday Fleur insisted again that I inhabit a woman and she inhabit a man. It was fun and exciting the first time. But the twenty-first? Repositioning oneself may bring some level of understanding but simply overturning the usual rules is not liberation, is not actually fixing things.

She sits stroking the soft white fibre-fur of our tame rat for ten or fifteen minutes at a time. I know that she is going a bit stir crazy. She has started to wonder what else we can project ourselves into. The computer console? The atmospheric cleansing machines? That noxious cloud outside?

Then she tells me that she wants to go into the panda.

I answer, "I know the animal experience is special but... you know the risks are so much greater."

"They shouldn't be," she moans, "it's basically the

same process. If we're stuck here forever, John, I want some variety or I'll go mad."

"You've had variety..." I whisper.

"And? Are you saying I should cease exploring, settle into the mousey life. That old suburban world of certainties is long gone. Destroyed – or hadn't you checked the sensors lately?"

"Let's not argue, Fleur. It doesn't achieve anything."

"Doesn't it? Maybe not with you. God, I wish I had someone else to argue with! Anyhow, all I wanted was a day being cute with big eyes and pretending to eat fake bamboo. It's not too much to ask, is it? You can sit and look after me. You'll find it... calming."

I acquiesce. I always do.

I believe that I recently dreamed for the first time in – how long? Weeks? Months? I may have actually been awake and hallucinating. Or completely lucid. Hard to tell.

My notion was that the polluted Earth beyond our shuttered windows and exits, the place known now to us only from sensor readings indicating temperature, humidity, atmospheric and terranean toxicity... all these were lies, fables with which we had fooled ourselves. The shocking truth was that we were really on a mission into deep space. The androids represented the vehicles through which we might explore these new horizons when we found them. There would be other... other choices, transports less conventional, lurking in some vault somewhere that we keep forgetting to check.

I know not whether there is any truth in this vision. We have no access to the world outside; or the void, if such it is.

Our mission has gone badly wrong. Crewmates, our Captain is dead. No god or authority figure to guide or save you. You've been left to your own devices from now on.

Maybe I could have saved Davidson. But I had started to suspect that instead of assisting us in all our transference desires, he was instead getting his voyeuristic kicks from seeing Fleur become a strong, virile man and take me quite forcibly when I was in female form. Or maybe he preferred it normal – me as a man, she as a woman, mechanically mating in apparent but exposed privacy. And what about the times we became animals? Did that pander to something unsavoury within his mindset?

I just miss the convenience of having a third, someone who could do the donkey work whilst Fleur and I flit from one host to another.

She has insisted on occupying the panda. All she has done is sit and rock from one haunch to the other whilst she acts out fake mastication. She looks at me with those doleful eyes which could melt the ice caps. If they weren't already mostly gone.

I have reasoned that the animal androids are a slightly lower grade than Rathfern's humanoid creations. This is why it's more difficult to effect transference in and out. I know that the risk element is part of the thrill for Fleur.

To me it doesn't seem much of a thrill to become an immobile black and white lump going nowhere and completing the same repeated actions over and over. Sure, her fur is soft and it's relaxing to let one's hand brush back and forth for a time. That's as far as it goes.

Maybe I'll be a little slow releasing her, keep her within the chosen animal body longer than she wishes. Think on that next time, Fleur.

The readings are exactly the same today as they were yesterday. I mean, not even one percentage out, not even a fraction of it. Surely things would vary a little bit one way or another? Even in a maelstrom, the gas is concentrated a shade more strongly here; the poison is a touch more toxic there. All things are changing in minute ways all the time, that's the nature of life.

Unless the readings are indeed false and, excuse the pun, a smokescreen.

I wish Rathfern was still here, he would know what to do.

Of course, he is still here in a way. The first victim of the failed transference. When I leave off caressing Fleur in her panda form I call over Professor Rat, gaze as deeply as I can into those red eyes, willing the trapped genius to find a way to communicate effectively. Maybe I should build him a maze, some sort of alphabetical labyrinth that he could race down to leave a linguistic trail behind.

At the very least, I could make a further effort to read his half a million words of notes off the computer screen and try to interpret them to my mundane self.

"Sorry, Rathfern," I mumble, "you should have chosen a worthier heir."

Machine failure again. This time I really will endeavour to fix the fault. Too much heartbreak and tragedy already, I can't stand any more.

Hold on, Fleur, I'll work out a way to release you.

Don't look at me so dolefully, it doesn't help the concentration any.

Allen Ashley works as a writer, poet, editor, critical reader, event host and writing tutor. He runs five creative writing groups in north London including the advanced group Clockhouse London Writers. His most recent books are as editor of Sensorama: Stories of the Senses (Eibonvale Press) and Creeping Crawlers (Shadow Publishing).

The Quarterly Review

Reviews by
Stephen Theaker,
Douglas J. Ogurek
and Jacob Edwards

Douglas J. Ogurek's work has appeared in the BFS Journal, The Literary Review, Morpheus Tales, Gone Lawn, and several anthologies. He lives in a Chicago suburb with the woman whose husband he is and their pit bull Phlegmpus Bilesnot. Douglas's website can be found at: www.douglasjogurek.weebly.com.

Jacob Edwards also writes 42-word reviews for Derelict Space Sheep. This writer, poet and recovering lexiphanicist's website is at www.jacobedwards.id.au. He also has a Facebook page at www.facebook.com/JacobEdwardsWriter, where he posts poems and the occasional oddity. Like him and follow him!

Audio

The Brenda and Effie Mysteries: Spicy Tea and Sympathy, by Paul Magrs (Bafflegab Productions)

Brenda, former bride of Frankenstein, tells most of this third story while strapped to a table in the murky underground base of a villain. Her blood is being drained and infused with a special tea, in hopes of bringing a dried-up corpse back to life. The situation dredges from the depths of Brenda's imperfect memory the events of a night in the fifties, when she worked as housemaid to Professor Tyler. He is one of the Smudglings, a group of fantasy writers much like the one frequented by C.S. Lewis and J.R.R. Tolkien. One of their meetings was disturbed by the attack of a

mummy, who made off with their best tea set and all
of its contents. In the present day this is somehow
connected with the Tipple teahouse (and massage
parlour), owned by international traveller and explorer
Professor Marius Keys, of whom Brenda says
"everything about him speaks of quality and polish", a
phrase that would be even more apt in description of
this series of audio plays. Anne Reid is terrific as
Brenda, bringing both the sweetness and the
toughness that the role requires, and the writing is a
constant delight, full of detail, care, specificity, and
ideas. Effie sounds uncannily like Sarah Millican,
which makes me smile every time she speaks. From
the moment the now familiar theme music plays, you
know it's going to be good. *Stephen Theaker* ★★★★☆

The Brenda and Effie Mysteries: Brenda Has Risen from the Grave, by Paul Magrs (Bafflegab Productions)

Effie might be in love, "in a whirlwind of amour" in
fact, with a man named Keith, who has an elephantine
proboscis upon his face. Brenda, former bride of
Frankenstein's monster, doesn't like Keith, and that
leads to a fall-out with Effie, who even stops opening
her little shop. As she worries about her friend,
memories return to Brenda of another old friend,
Joseph Merrick, known as the Elephant Man back
when they were in a travelling circus together. She was
the Half-Dead Woman, who could let her stitches
loose and horrify the crowds by wriggling her bits
when they weren't attached to each other any more.
She was a callow young thing then, less than a century
old, and just like Effie she didn't listen to the advice of
a well-meaning friend when she should have. What's
more, women were being killed back then, and they
are dying now as well in a very similar way. It's too

soon for Brenda and Effie to go their separate ways. We learn much more about Brenda in this story (at least those of us who haven't read more than one or two of the original novels yet). She has been in the course of her long life "a graverobber, a vagabond, a woman of ill repute, a warrior, a witch, a handmaiden to a queen, a sorcerer's assistant, a lady pirate" and one suspects that isn't all, but what she needs to be in this fourth story is a good friend, and perhaps she's better at that than anything else. Another entertaining story, though it's rather less light-hearted than earlier instalments. *Stephen Theaker* ★★★☆☆

Doctor Who and the Ark in Space, by Ian Marter (BBC/Audible)

The fourth Doctor, only recently regenerated and accompanied by journalist Sarah Jane Smith and U.N.I.T. medic Harry Sullivan, lands the Tardis on the Nerva Beacon. It seems to be abandoned, but further investigation reveals slimy trails, as if of a giant slug, and then freeze-dried humans, packed away in storage for thousands of years to survive a stellar disaster. The first humans to wake up suspect the Tardis crew of sabotage, a fatal distraction from their true, hidden enemies: the Wirrn, a race of giant locust-like insects with a grudge against humanity, and a gruesome purpose for these survivors. "The Ark in Space" was originally a television story, and this is the Audible version of the Target novelisation from the eighties, written by the actor who played Harry Sullivan. He wasn't in the Tardis long, sadly, having been cast as the Chestertonian man of action, an entirely redundant position after Tom Baker took the role of the Doctor. It is read by *Dead Ringers* star Jon Culshaw, who first became famous for his wonderful telephone impersonations of Tom Baker's Doctor. That ability

makes him perfect for this audiobook, though
ironically this comes from a time when the fourth
Doctor wasn't particularly funny – for much of this
story he's indistinguishable from his previous, rather
serious, incarnation. He narrates in his own reading
voice, and keeps the tension high. For a children's
book it is surprisingly gory, with talk of suppurating
stumps and smouldering bodies welded to panelling
after being repeatedly shot, and in the audio version
there's no bubble wrap to break the spell. Sarah Jane's
long, arduous and essential crawl through a narrow
duct is as stressful as ever, no matter how many times
we've already seen her succeed. The fate of one human
infected by the Wirrn bears repetition in full: "with a
crack, like a gigantic seedpod bursting, his whole head
split open. A fountain of green froth erupted and came
sizzling down the radiation suit..." There's a reason

these were my favourites as a child: other books were, quite literally, bloodless in comparison. *Stephen Theaker* ★★★☆☆

Doctor Who: Echoes of Grey, by John Dorney (Big Finish)

This sixty-seven minute play checks in with Zoe Heriot, now in her fifties after being returned to her own time by the Time Lords. They wiped her memories of her travels with the Doctor, leaving her with just the recollection of his visit to the Wheel in Space to fight the Cybermen, but she has an eidetic memory, and she can tell that there's a discontinuity in her mind. It has made it difficult to form relationships; she feels like the ghost of herself. Then she meets Ally Monroe, whose life she apparently saved during one of the adventures she can't remember. Ally thinks her alpha wave gadget will help, and slowly Zoe starts to remember the time she, Jamie and the second Doctor encountered the Achromatics, grey beings who declare their love for you while draining away your life. It's a second Doctor story in the classic style, of slow-moving monsters in a confined space, with all the creepiness that brings. When they chase the Doctor around a room (he has a plan, but "no other ideas at all!") it's easy to imagine how it would have looked on screen. Wendy Padbury is as adept at voicing the Doctor and Jamie as when playing her younger self. The framing device is cleverly done, and by the time it ends the play's title turns out to be clever too. It's a good story, though its ramifications are potentially tragic: if Zoe and – as we've learned in other stories – Jamie have recovered some of their memories, did the Doctor make a terrible mistake in the Tomb of Rassilon? *Stephen Theaker* ★★★☆☆

Doctor Who: The Guardian of the Solar System, by Simon Guerrier (Big Finish)

The first story in the fifth series of the Companion Chronicles sees the return for seventy-one minutes of Sara Kingdom (Jean Marsh). Well, sort of. On television she helped the first Doctor defeat the Daleks' master-plan, and paid the ultimate price. Here, what appears to be a digital copy of her mind has lived on for a thousand years as the host of a guest house with remarkable properties. As the house Sara healed the sick daughter of a man named Robert (Niall MacGregor), and in return he promised to stay there forever, not realising perhaps that forever in that house would be a long time indeed. He has one last thing to ask of her, but before she will hear his request she wants to tell him one last story, a side-quest during her time with the Doctor and space pilot Steven Tyler, when they travelled back in time to discover the dark secret at the heart of the human empire, what powers their flight to the stars. Along the way, she got the chance to meet Bret Vyon, the brother she would betray, when he was still alive. It's a good story with tender, emotional performances, and a melancholy, downbeat feel, about people caught in the wheels of time, trying to escape the inevitable, trying to escape the past. *Stephen Theaker* ★★★☆☆

Vince Cosmos: Glam Rock Detective, by Paul Magrs (Bafflegab Productions)

January 1972, and Poppy Munday (played by Lauren Kellegher) moves down to London, where she feels at first like she's living in a movie. She moves in with a friend, but then struggles to find work, and her favourite pop star is shot while playing live on radio. Things are getting a bit miserable before she gets a

frantic call from her mum back home: Poppy has won
a competition to attend the launch of *Galactic Cinders*,
the new album by her favourite, Vince Cosmos. He's a
lot like Bowie/Ziggy, full of facets and wearing make-
up and feeling the zeitgeist and talking about the
cosmic godhead. Weirdly, the creepy, angry little man
who lives in the flat above hers is at the launch too. Is
he there to assassinate Vince? This two-part story feels
like a pilot, in that we're a long time into the story
before we finally get to spend time with Vince himself.
I expected to love Julian Rhind-Tutt in this – he was
brilliant as a similarly foppish character in the highly
underrated sitcom *Hippies* – but somehow it doesn't
quite work, maybe because it doesn't feel like he
believes the more pretentious Bowie-like utterances of
his character. He's knowing when he should be
oblivious. He does a good job with Vince's songs,

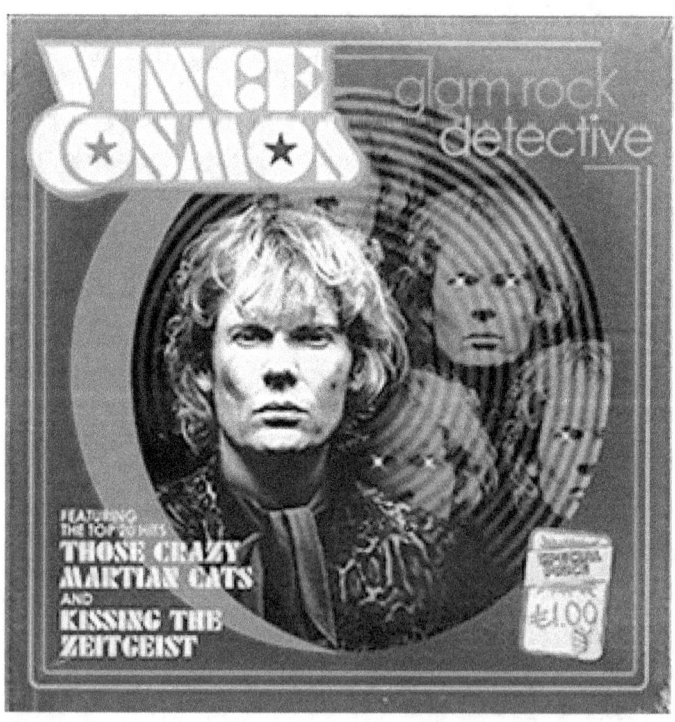

though, and by the end I wished that he'd been in it more. I also enjoyed the links to a classic piece of sf literature, and to the Brenda and Effie stories: the ventriloquist's fuzzy bat out of hell shows up here at a royal variety performance, still in his pomp. *Stephen Theaker* ★★★☆☆

Books

An Occupation of Angels, by Lavie Tidhar (Apex Publications)

Secret agent Killarney pursues a cryptographer, Dr Eldershott, across cold war Europe, fighting enemy agents on the Trans-Siberian Express and discovering secret bases carved out of rock. But this isn't the world of James Bond. Thirty-five years ago the angels came, and now their obese bodies lounge within places like Notre Dame and Saint Paul's while the angels extend their influence over human affairs. At least until the assassinations begin. Who is behind the killings, and what is the being that occupies Sophie Stockard's body, and speaks in such a terrible voice? Killarney has some experience of angel-killing herself, but must stop this wave of deaths before the balance of power is broken and the cold war goes hot. Yet another good novella by Lavie Tidhar. The pace is fast, jumps in time making each chapter begin with a snap, and there are surprises and new ideas all the way through. Killarney herself seems to have secrets that are only hinted at here. *Stephen Theaker* ★★★☆☆

The Bureau of Them, by Cate Gardner (Spectral Press)

Glynn has been dead for thirteen months, twelve days,

seven hours and some minutes, and Katy can't stop missing him, can't move on with her life. She doesn't want to. He walked out in front of a coach, so there's no doubt about his passing, but she thinks she sees him watching her, and these brief glimpses lead her to an abandoned office building, where dust and shadows move with uncanny life. Glynn has become part of this office of lost souls, the bureau of them, and they are looking for new recruits! As in previous books like *In*

By Cate Gardner

the Broken Birdcage of Kathleen Fair and *Nowhere Hall*
Cate Gardner creates an eerie atmosphere that serves
the story well, and Katy's grief is painful to watch. For
me it was a bit disappointing that there wasn't more
bureaucracy in the novella, the title conjuring up
visions of weird, secret officialdom working behind
the scenes of reality, and that isn't really what it's
about, the office here being more of a base than where
the work is done. (I'm trying to avoid giving too much
away.) The novella's spell is broken a bit by a couple of
jarring production problems: "may" being used
instead of "might" all the way through, and (in the
ebook at least) unspaced hyphens being used in place
of dashes, which leaves the reader trying to make
sense of odd hyphenates (e.g. "Sounds echoed from
within the cinema-tinny"). Definitely worth reading,
though. No other writer I've read is producing books
that remind me so very much of my own bad dreams.
If Cate Gardner's next book is about being lost in a
spooky school without a timetable you'll know she's
stolen my dream journal. *Stephen Theaker* ★★★☆☆

Doctor Who: The Angel's Kiss, by Melody Malone (BBC Books)

River Song is in New York, working as a private eye
under the name Melody Malone, just as we found her
at the beginning of the television episode, "The Angels
Take Manhattan". She takes the case of a minor film
star, Rock Railton, who has overheard someone saying
that he will die. Then she runs into a fellow who looks
like him on the street, dying, and extremely old. At a
party she meets him again, young and beautiful but
without the slightest idea who she is. Weird stuff is
going on and she wants to figure it out whether she
gets paid or not. This short book, written in truth by
Justin Richards, doesn't match the passages quoted

from it on television, sadly, but it does lead nicely into that story, and it gives River Song a lot of fun things to say and do. The audio version, read by Alex Kingston herself, must be a hoot. *Stephen Theaker* ★★★☆☆

Doctor Who: City of Death by Douglas Adams and James Goss, from a story by David Fisher (BBC Books)

The gamble with time – playing the odds of authorship.

Douglas Adams' involvement with *Doctor Who* is... complicated. For many years the three scripts he wrote were lamented as being very good (*City of Death*), very bad (*The Pirate Planet*), very good *and* bad in a Schrödinger's cat kind of way (the unfinished, unbroadcast *Shada*), and in all cases very much and quite pointedly so, unnovelised. Adams did write a fourth script, which *was* novelised, but that was *Doctor Who and the Krikkitmen*, which upon being rejected by the *Doctor Who* production team eventually lost the Doctor and regenerated into Adams' third *Hitchhiker's* novel, *Life, the Universe and Everything*. In a similar vein, *City of Death* and *Shada* weren't *entirely* unnovelised: significant portions of them found their way into *Dirk Gently's Holistic Detective Agency*. But these caveats aside, of all the authors whose stories could have disappeared into the time void, it was Adams alone (okay, and two of Eric Saward's scripts; not such a great loss) whose *Who* output was destined not to line the bookshelves of fans most eager to devour it. Adams wouldn't accept the pittance being offered by Target Books; nor, especially after he'd cherry-picked from them himself, would he allow his scripts to be novelised by someone else. End of story.

Well, not quite. A decade after Douglas Adams' tragically premature death, his estate relented and

gave permission for Gareth Roberts to work on *Shada*.
The resulting novel, which is quite brilliantly executed,
is probably the only fleck of silver in the dark cloud of
Adams' passing. It also paved the way for two more
posthumous collaborations, with Roberts' next
assignment being *City of Death*. Which he now hasn't

written. Instead, the cover credits Douglas Adams and
James Goss, from a story by David Fisher.
Complicated? Just a little.

Upon broadcast, *City of Death* was ascribed to
David Agnew, which was a BBC pseudonym used to
cover up the similarly trifold mixed parentage of
Adams, producer Graham Williams and the
aforementioned David Fisher, who was unavailable
when money was scrounged to film abroad and his
original script (*The Gamble With Time*) needed a last-
minute reworking to accommodate a location shoot in
Paris. Adams, who as script editor was at least partly
responsible for letting this potential crisis reach the
eleventh hour, consequently was locked up over the
course of a weekend and, with Williams now script-
editing, rattled off *City of Death*. The resulting story,
compared to, say, the analogously last-minute *So Long,
and Thanks for All the Fish*, was a triumph. David
Fisher's script provided the perfect framework for
Adamsishness at its most piquant, to which was added
the splendour of Paris, a certain bonhomie of
performance by Tom Baker, Lalla Ward and guest
stars, and also an ITV strike that *ipso facto* sent the
BBC viewing figures skywards. From rather troubled
beginnings, *City of Death* thus became officially (and
in many eyes unofficially) the most popular *Doctor
Who* story of the original series. Now, fast forward
thirty-five years or so and—

Enter, James Goss, who, true to the spirit of the
original penning (albeit perhaps lacking the panache
to pull it off) was drafted in to write the novel when
Gareth Roberts proved suddenly and unexpectedly
unavailable. Notwithstanding the task still awaiting
whomever is ordained worthy of bringing *The Pirate
Planet* from screen to page, surely this must go down
as the toughest if potentially most rewarding

enterprise ever gifted a *Who* novelist. And the result? Well, it's complicated...

Shada tells the story of Scaroth, last of the Jagaroth, who fell splintered through time when his spaceship exploded back at the dawn of Earth's history, and has been working ever since to advance humanity to the point of civilisation whereby Count Scarlioni, the last of his personas, can invent a time machine and travel back to prevent himself from initiating the calamity in the first place. To fund his experiments, Scarlioni is planning to steal the Mona Lisa and then sell off the multiple copies he's arranged an earlier fragment of himself to commission from Leonardo Da Vinci. The only people standing in his way are the Doctor and Romana, who have come to Paris for a holiday, and Duggan, a pugilistic detective whose fist-happy approach provides both a semi-satirical contrast to the Doctor's methods and an unerring source of humorous material. Punches and *bon mots* abound. Unfortunately, in the novel, so does the unconscionable shrapnel of typographical mishap. The book, simply put, hasn't been proofread, which is something of a recurring issue in the BBC range but exacerbated in this instance by the hasty composition. It's a terrible shame for a glossy hardcover bearing Douglas Adams' name. As to the writing itself...

James Goss starts with a chapter of jumbled vignettes, which ostensibly lend backstory to all the characters (however minor) who appear in the televised version of *City of Death*, but which serve also the purpose of obfuscating the reader's connection to the original. This isn't a bad idea — let the novel stand for itself, Goss says, not merely call to mind memories of what most readers will already have seen — yet he then presents a narrative that *does*, particularly in its descriptive elements, rely on that prior knowledge. For example: Douglas Adams contrived for John Cleese and Eleanor Bron to make a cameo appearance in the art gallery scene towards the end of episode four. This was loved by some viewers, criticised by others, but in either case was something of a throwaway. For Goss to have seeded this cameo with several other Cleese/Bron showings earlier in the novel is pointless at best and at worst tripping the light nonsensical for anyone approaching the book as a self-contained entity. Other characters are fleshed out more purposefully, adding at least to the overall mood, if not strictly speaking to the story itself, but the approach is patchy. Goss does afford more substance to the Doctor and Romana than is evident on screen, but even here, where the veneer of flippancy is peeled back to reveal more serious layers beneath, the effect is spoiled somewhat by an unkempt narrative glibness that comes and goes but overall seems hell-bent on crafting a *Hitchhiker's* pastiche. This is something Gareth Roberts efficaciously avoided in *Shada*, whereas in *City of Death* the stylistic aping is not only evident but also unnervingly off-kilter; if Adams' narrative voice were to have been evoked, the darker, more measured timbre of *Dirk Gently* would surely have been a better choice.

   James Goss has obviously approached his task with diligence and enthusiasm, taking pains not only to bring the televised story to life but also to ascertain those of Adams' intentions that didn't make the transition from script to screen, and to work these into the finished product. Thus, for instance, Scarlioni's gratuitous end-of-episode reveal as Scaroth is explained at last, as to some extent is the conjugal oddity by which the Countess Scarlioni has never quite noticed that her husband is (in every sense, but especially physically, albeit behind a mask) not human. Other inconsistencies remain the unexplored purview of dramatic licence; and perhaps rightly so, for to probe them more deeply would achieve nothing more than to detract from a tale fizzing with exuberance. Goss has had to strike a balance between presenting *City of Death* "as is" and remodelling it as something that more intricately wasn't; between showing due reverence to the spirit of Douglas Adams and due respect to the need to look beyond him. Aforesaid misgivings aside, he's managed the feat quite well; and although the James Goss novelisation might sit as third-placed iteration on the multiverse podium, below the gold and silver of those by Adams and Roberts, nevertheless it is a book worth slotting into what otherwise would remain just a wistfully set-aside space on the shelf. *Jacob Edwards*

None of Our Yesterdays, by Vaughan Stanger (self-published)

Two fine stories of alternative history in a nice little ebook. In "The Peace Criminal", which first appeared in *Postscripts*, a television producer and his researcher interview a strange old man who remembers what happened in England after Germany won World War I. At first they think his story might make a good episode of *Myths and Mysteries of the Twentieth Century* for the History Channel, but his story is more disturbing than expected. "The Eyepatch Protocol" (which after reading the story one realises is a fantastic title) follows a bomber crew tasked with retaliation after the Cuban missile crisis leads Krushchev to launch his missiles. (Weird to remember how a phrase like "four-minute warning" haunted my childhood, when now I shout it to let the kids know their dinner is almost ready.) It's shorter than the first story. but equally powerful. *Stephen Theaker* ★★★★☆

On a Red Station, Drifting, by Aliette de Bodard (Nine Dragons River)

The Great Virtue Emperor is losing control of the star-spanning Dai Viet Empire. Rebels like Lord Soi are tearing it apart. Linh, the highly educated magistrate of the Twenty-Third Planet, was induced to flee before it fell to the war-kites of the rebel lords. The shame of that flight is bad enough, but she also sent a strongly-worded report on the civil war to the Emperor, which some might see as treasonous in its questioning of his leadership abilities. Le Thi Quyen is the administrator of Prosper Station, working with the Mind – the Honoured Ancestress – who controls its every function. As well as the arrival of Linh and all the danger that brings, she must investigate the apparent malfunctioning of the Honoured Ancestress and the betrayal of her own brother, Huu Hieu, who sold off the memory chips containing the thoughts of their revered ancestors. The station's Mind helps its inhabitants to cope with the unnaturality of life in space, sharing their thoughts and cloaking the metal and rivets with poetry and decoration, but as she loses her strength, the comfort and connection she provides ebbs away, putting the lives of everyone on the station in the hands of Linh and Quyen, and at the mercy of their quarrel. This novella is imaginative and intense, each character stretched to their breaking point, many spouses missing in the war, now struggling to cope with current crises while knowing that worse is to come, fighting their own worst impulses when the wrong word at the wrong time could be fatal. *Stephen Theaker* ★★★★☆

Slow Bullets, by Alastair Reynolds
(Tachyon Publications)

There was a war between the Central Worlds and the Peripheral Systems, both of them fairly religious, and just as a peace was agreed Scurelya Timsuk Shunde, our narrator, is captured by a war criminal and taken to a bunker, where he injects her with a slow bullet, which'll burrow through her body till it reaches her heart. She's left to die, and probably will, and then she wakes up...

Now, I was glad to be able to read the book and be surprised by everything that came next, and if you want the full effect too then skip to the star rating and buy the book. If not...

She wakes up on a damaged skipship, with a tiny crew, which had been transporting soldiers from both sides of the war. They seem to have arrived, but the world below is unfamiliar, the waking passengers are beginning to riot, and Scurelya thinks she sees her torturer among them. What's more, there is now an unfamiliar ship docked at the airlock. This is a very good novella, each step Scur takes teaching us something new, about her, the ship, the universe she lives in. Perhaps those revelations won't all come as a surprise to existing fans of Alastair Reynolds' work, but it hits the new reader all at once. The tension and mystery and thoughtfulness reminded me of *Journey into Space*, where Jet Morgan and his team would so often find themselves exploring an unfamiliar, curious spaceship with a dangerous occupant. The situation has no obvious answers, so the reader is led to think things through with Scur and the allies she begins to gather, and to see how culture can be borne out of necessity. *Stephen Theaker* ★★★★☆

Comics

Barbarella, Book 1, by Jean-Claude Forest (Humanoids)

I'm always amazed at how little I like the film *Barbarella*, given how much I generally adore that kind of sci-fi from the sixties and seventies. I think the problem is just that it's dull. This is not a charge you could level at the original comic book, presented here

in a new English-language adaptation by Kelly Sue DeConnick of *Captain Marvel* fame. It's too random and fast-moving to be dull, bouncing from one over-the-top scenario to another like a hyperactive moon-man. Barbarella is a space traveller whose tried and trusted approach to danger is to take off all her clothes, though to be fair that usually works out for her, and she's uncynical about using her charms that way. She's spaced-out, disengaged, lusty, bisexual, and looks a lot like Brigitte Bardot. Her adventures in this first book include encounters with flower growers under siege, a face-thief, a hunter and the scientist who creates monsters for him to fight, the Princesses of Yesteryear and my personal greatest fear, flying sharks! At its best it reminds me of our own much-missed Newton Braddell, and even at its worst it's enjoyable. Despite the sauciness, it doesn't feel adult in tone. In art and narrative style it reminds me rather of the lightweight, sketchy stories that would appear in children's annuals from the sixties, like those for Doctor Who and Bleep and Booster, just with rather saltier content in places. It ends very abruptly, but that feels okay. It's not the greatest comic you'll ever read. I do think it's worth reading. *Stephen Theaker* ★★★☆☆

Doctor Who: The Good Soldier, by Andrew Cartmel, Mike Collins and chums (Panini Comics)

A 128pp collection of strips from *Doctor Who Magazine* issues 164 to 179, plus a couple from specials, and a pair of text stories. This is the third collection of stories featuring the seventh Doctor, as played by Sylvester McCoy, not the easiest of Doctors to draw, and the twentieth Panini collection overall. As ever with this series of books, the reproduction of the artwork is flawless, as is the overall presentation. Unlike *Nemesis of the Daleks*, the previous seventh

Doctor collection, this doesn't include any sub-par strips from *The Incredible Hulk Presents*. It gets off to a great start with "Fellow Travellers", illustrated by Arthur Ranson. "The Mark of Mandragora", in which the malevolent and ancient intelligence manipulates the Doctor and the Tardis, has previously been collected in a Marvel graphic novel, but it's not a patch on the title story, "The Good Soldier", by Andrew Cartmel and Mike Collins, where the Doctor and Ace encounter the original Mondasian Cybermen on a trip to 1954 Nevada. In its look and feel it points towards how consistently ambitious the strip would become during the eighth Doctor's tenure. The commentary section is as fascinating as ever. My very favourite panel of the book makes the writer of that story cringe! And did you know that Andrew Cartmel approached Alan Moore to write for the television programme? *Stephen Theaker* ★★★☆☆

**Empowered, Vol. 8, by Adam Warren
(Dark Horse Books)**

Sistah Spooky is still devastated by the loss of her lover, and it's made all the worse by her having kept their relationship secret during their time together. Emp is feeling terrible about it too, wondering if she could have done something different on the Superhomeys' space station D10. So the two of them do something really stupid that involves using forbidden alien weaponry (forbidden because six years ago it created a new volcano in San Antonio) to batter at the gates of hell. We'll learn lots more about Sistah Spooky and even a bit about Emp's unfortunate tendency to get tied up by supervillains. This book keeps up the high standards of the series. From an unpromising beginning Emp has grown into one of the bravest, most admirable and most determined superheroes in comics. I may have only bought the whole series because it was on sale at Dark Horse Digital (it was Father's Day and I deserved a treat!), but it's now a solid favourite of mine. The stories take a while to bloom, but when they do you care because the roots go so deep. *Stephen Theaker* ★★★★☆

Empowered: Unchained, Vol. 1, by Adam Warren and chums (Dark Horse Books)

Collects various one-shots about Empowered, most of them featuring a colour section drawn by a guest artist. One special is all about Maidman, who dresses as a maid and thus casts more fear into the hearts of criminals than anyone dressed as a bat would ever do. In others: a horny robot's cyberfantasies run riot in a dump for the detritus of superhero battles; Ninjette explains the nine stages of her drunkenness; Empowered fights a gang of animal-themed superheroes, and explains how much more useful cars can be in battle if you don't just throw them at your enemies; and Empowered and Ninjette take a fantastic voyage into an alien baby who is bigger on the inside. *Stephen Theaker* ★★★★☆

Forever Evil, by Geoff Johns, David Finch and Richard Friend (DC Comics)

After the superheroes get sucked into Firestorm, that leaves just Batman and the supervillains, led by Lex Luthor in his seventies-chic power-armour, to fight off an invasion from another dimension! It's the Crime Syndicate of America, evil mirrors of the Justice League like Ultraman and Superwoman, fleeing the destruction of their own world. Most of the villains are happy to join the Crime Syndicate in ruling the world, but Captain Cold, Black Manta, Sinestro, Catwoman

and Lex's newly decanted Bizarro will join Lex (and
Batman) in taking them down. For a big DC event this
has a tight focus for the most part, the confrontation
taking place within a downed JLA watchtower by the
sea. The art to my eyes isn't very attractive, a bit
rougher than I prefer, but I suppose that fits with us
seeing the world from a villain's point of view. Batman
looks good. Sinestro comes across very well, his
method of dealing with the cowardly Power Ring
being particularly decisive. *Stephen Theaker* ★★★☆☆

The Glorkian Warrior and the Mustache of Destiny, by James Kochalka (First Second)

The funniest idiot since Groo the Wanderer returns for his third "adventure". That is to say, he has a nightmare about a giant moustache, decides that he has invented a talking coffee cup, gets headbutted by a bunch of armless baby would-be Glorkian Warriors, and falls down a big hole. Later, he falls down another hole and meets the book's villain, Quackaboodle the Space God! (Although I have my qualms about the behaviour of the Glorkian Supergrandma too.) This is just as funny as the previous two books, the stupidity reaching absolutely glorious levels, e.g. the four baby Glorks saying, "Can Gonk do *this*?" and "Can Doonkies do thats?" and "May Crazy Face?" and then "Cans Bronk bronk bronk?" In context it's funny, trust me, on this if nothing else. And while we're talking about glorious, you should see the colours in this book. You know that nonsense about using 10% of your brain? The art in this book makes you feel like you've only been using 10% of your eyes. A thank you page at the end makes it sound like this may be the last in the series. Let's hope not. I could keep reading these forever. It's not out till March 2016, so don't let your children grow up too fast. *Stephen Theaker* ★★★★★

Green Lantern: The Sinestro Corps War, by Geoff Johns, Ethan van Sciver and chums (DC Comics)

This is a story from what I think of as the "real" DC universe, the time between *Crisis on Infinite Earths*, to which this book is in many ways a sequel, and *Flashpoint*, which reset everything for the New 52 universe. For a long time before the crisis the DC heroes lived, like Archie or the Bash Street Kids, in an eternal golden present, but a Teen Titan called Robin wanted to grow up, and he couldn't do that unless other people got older, and so time began to flow. The hair of Green Lantern Hal Jordan went grey at the temples, and during *The Return of Superman* he lost his mind, after Mongol and the cyborg Superman destroyed his home Coast City while building a base. He betrayed the Green Lantern Corps, became the villain Parallax, and gave his life to save the world from the Final Night, the attack of a sun-eater. What a life! But it wasn't over! He then became the new Spectre (god's spirit of vengeance) but it didn't stick, and eventually, like so many Silver Age heroes, he too returned from the grave, to lead the Green Lantern Corps once again, his misdeeds as Parallax retconned as a kind of possession by a fear monster by that name.

The problem with Hal is that for all the affection in which he's held and the tumultuous events of his life, he tends to be quite a dull, flavourless character – presumably the reason they replaced him in the first place. This book surrounds him with other Green Lanterns to prevent that being a problem. Long-time GLs John Stewart, Guy Gardner and Kyle Rayner all play prominent roles, but this is about the Green Lantern Corps as a whole, fighting a huge war against its most terrible threat. Sinestro, once the greatest Green Lantern of them all, has been recruiting his own yellow corps, of villains who have the power to inspire fear. At his side are the cyborg Superman Hank Henshaw, deranged survivor of the Crisis Superboy-Prime, and the Anti-Monitor himself, plus thousands of other recruits.

Even Hal Jordan couldn't make this book boring. It's a true epic in the style of the earlier books it draws on, the kind of thing that would usually be a company-wide crossover. There are a hundred things happening on every page, deaths by the dozen, the story taking place in amongst a blizzard of green and yellow rings searching for worthy new owners. The issues collected here are from two titles, *Green Lantern* and *Green Lantern Corps*, not that you could tell, the story holding together so well. The collection does something that is much too rare in DC's books – each

chapter identifies the original issue it came from, and provides the individual writers and artists and the original title of that story, so you know exactly what you're reading. The artwork throughout is very good, the amount of work that must have gone into each panel quite staggering. Almost any page of it would make an epic poster. I can't think of a Green Lantern story I liked more. The battle between the vicious Superman-Prime (as he's now called) and a Daxamite Green Lantern who can almost match him in strength is brilliantly brutal. I also liked the way that the real Superman shows up in the big battles at the end but doesn't get to speak, because it isn't his comic. And yet my very favourite bit, in this interplanetary, intergalactic, *interuniversal* war, was the littlest: Green Lantern Leezle Pon, a superintelligent smallpox virus. *Stephen Theaker* ★★★★☆

Invincible, Vol. 18: The Death of Everyone, by Robert Kirkman, Ryan Ottley and Cliff Rathburn (Image Comics/Skybound)

Mark Grayson, aka Invincible, is an extremely strong and durable (albeit not indestructible) superhero who inherited his powers from his father, an alien who was originally hanging around on Earth with a view to making it a part of his people's empire. As this volume begins, Invincible's powers are on the blink, and Zandale, the hero formerly known as Bulletproof, has been keeping his costume warm. But Zandale is about to make the mistake of telling his parents his astonishing origin story, and Mark will discover that sometime ally, more often enemy Dinosaurus has been making big plans. It's a shocking book from start to finish, as you might expect from the collection that spans this comic's hundredth issue. That's one of the things I love about this comic, its scope for telling those huge stories: it's as if *Crisis on Infinite Earths*, *Civil War*, *Infinite Crisis*, *The Death of Superman* and *Zero Hour* all happened in the same ongoing series. The status quo can be completely upended in *Invincible* – and in this volume it does, a good half dozen times – without concern for the effect upon twenty other books that feature the same character. This isn't the remixed version of a story I've read three times already, and when Mark's friends are in danger there's every chance that they could really die. That's why I'm up to volume eighteen of this when I haven't even reached *issue* eighteen of a new DC or Marvel universe book in years. *Stephen Theaker* ★★★☆☆

Olympus, Book #1, by Geoff Johns, Kris Grimminger and Butch Guice (Humanoids)

Professor Walker and her assistant Brent are on a dive, ten miles off the coast of Thessaly, when they discover a sunken galley, and inside the galley a sealed trunk. Back on board their ship, the *Desmon*, with student sisters Rebecca and Sarah, they must decide whether to open it. The right thing to do would be to notify the Greek authorities, but Brent reminds the professor of the dean's plan to close the archaeology department... They open it, and inside is an ancient urn, bearing the inscription, "Herein contains the misfortunes of man." Could it be Pandora's box? Even as they think about that, a storm whips up around them, just in time to accompany a gang of gun-toting pirates who expect to find diamonds on board. The storm doesn't stop till the *Desmon* is washed up on the shores of a paradise island, with a giant statue of naked Zeus on the beach. More adventures ensue! This is a very good-looking book, Dan Brown's colouring looking especially good in the digital format. Bikini-wearing Sarah's tendency to find a new pose for each panel seems a bit cheesy, but the mysterious island is as spectacular as the plot needs it to be. The central idea is interesting, even if the way events play out, at least in this first book, is the same as any number of films – the book feels like it was made with both eyes on Hollywood. The story stops on a cliffhanger (when most of the characters are asleep), so it doesn't feel like a complete album in itself, but it's still very enjoyable. I especially liked the sound effect used here when a guy gets punched in the jaw: "PLAF!" *Stephen Theaker* ★★★☆☆

Planetary Brigade, by J.M. DeMatteis, Keith Giffen, Julia Bax and chums (BOOM! Studios)

The Planetary Brigade is a team of mismatched superheroes from the writers of *Justice League International*. Captain Valour, the Grim Knight and Earth Mother are analogues of Superman, Batman and Wonder Woman, the first two played for laughs, as if the chummy Superman of the fifties teamed up with the Batman of the nineties. Purring Pussycat is a former supervillain who joined the team after becoming disenchanted with mentor Mister Master, two feuding brothers in one body who will destroy the world if he can't conquer it. Mister Brilliant is an obese genius in a weaponised hoverchair who runs a comic book store in his spare time.

The standout characters are the Third Eye, the team's female Phantom Stranger/John Constantine/Doctor Strange, and the Mauve Visitor, an ambi-sexual acerbic alien with a taste for the finer things in life.

The book is a bit of a jumble, collecting a two-issue series illustrated by several artists in each issue and a three-issue series that jumps around the group's timeline. On the whole it works, and though the art styles change from page to page it's all good. It's not as funny as the JLI, but I devoured dozens of issues of that comic all at once so there was time for the running jokes to hit top speed. A scene at the end hits a bum note, where a kiss with a trans character is said to be less scandalous because she's has sex-change surgery. Not my place to forgive it that clumsiness, but at least the book is *trying* to be progressive and accepting.

A more cohesive follow-up with a longer present-day adventure for the team would be very welcome.

Stephen Theaker ★★★☆☆

The Red Seas, Book One: Under the Banner of King Death: The Complete Digital Edition, by Ian Edginton and Steve Yeowell (Rebellion)

Captain Jack Dancer got his ship by leading a mutiny, outraged by the mistreatment of the crew. Now he leads them to adventure on the high seas. They are treated a bit better, but their chances of survival haven't improved. This book collects three of their adventures. In the first they must do battle with Dr

Orlando Doyle, a hollow man with a crew of the dead. In the second they meet Aladdin, in search of Laputa and still giving orders to his genie, and in the third they travel deep within the earth, where a beautiful empress rules a race of lizard men. Three other stories feature people met by Jack Dancer on his travels: Sir Isaac Newton (his life secretly extended by the Brotherhood) fights a British war criminal possessed by an ancient Roman demigod; the two-headed dog Erebus (having left one head at home) and a friend hunt hidden treasures in blitz-torn London; and the regulars of Jack's favourite watering hole must deal with a fellow who is "much more than a man... and a little less than *God*". It's three hundred and seventy pages of unapologetic adventure, made all the more satisfying by being drawn in its black-and-white entirety by Steve Yeowell. (I still remember how disappointed I was when I realised he wouldn't be illustrating the whole of *The Invisibles*.) The stories were originally serialised in brief episodes in *2000 AD*, but apart from Isaac Newton's werewolf fight (which features little diary recaps) they are seamless, each of the three main stories reading like a short graphic novel. It's a digital-only collection, so look out for it in the *2000 AD* app and places like that. *Stephen Theaker*
★★★☆☆

Redhand: Twilight of the Gods, Book 1: Son of Oblivion, by Kurt Busiek and Mario Alberti (with an epilogue by Sam Timel and Bazal) (Humanoids)

A party of highly religious, spear-carrying hunters stumble across a strange place while fleeing Kiotha slavers. It contains many dead bodies suspended in liquid within green tubes. But as the slavers attack, it turns out that one of the men in the tubes lives! He emerges naked, and fights mindlessly, but elegantly,

like an automaton. Afterwards, his first words to the
hunters become his name, because he doesn't know
who he is: "Red... hand..." Returning to their home, he
faces the usual problems of the man with no name
after the battle is done: hardly anyone wants him to
stick around – except the pretty girl, and she has a
jealous and angry admirer. This is a beautifully drawn
graphic novel, every panel full of detail and interest.
The story is one we've heard before, but it never gets
old, and this version takes some surprising turns as it

progresses. This should appeal greatly to anyone who yearns for new stories in the style of the early Elric books. *Stephen Theaker* ★★★★☆

Superman: Doomed, by Greg Pak and chums (DC Comics)

A young Superman is dating Wonder Woman rather than Lois Lane, and maybe that's a good thing because Lois is currently under the control of Brainiac, who is in deep space, preparing to add the people of Earth to his collection. That would be trouble enough, but what's more Doomsday, the monstrous product of Kryptonian science, has been resurrected, this time with the brand new ability to drain the life from anything nearby. (It isn't clear whether Doomsday has killed Superman yet in this new reality.) Superman decides that there's only one way to stop the monster for good, and rips it to bits, and then, erm, inhales what's left, and is thus infected himself. He has Doomsday's rage, strength, bony bits, and tendency to suck the life out of a room. How to fight off Brainiac's attack when it's not safe for the Man of Steel to be on Earth any more? This is a chunky five hundred page book on Comixology, though in print it would be even longer because all the double page spreads count as one page each on Comixology. It's surprising to see so many of them here: they are a pest to read on a tablet (and don't look much better in a print collection). It's almost like print issue devotees are deliberately throwing their clogs in the digital works. The book collects material from eight different titles, including five issues each of *Action Comics* and *Superman/Wonder Woman*, and there are sections where the art style changes every few pages; it's a jigsaw where each piece was drawn by a different person, but somehow it hangs together pretty well. It's quite contrived, since so much of the story hangs on Superman acquiring powers from Doomsday that Doomsday doesn't usually have. Perhaps it was felt that involving Parasite in the story wouldn't have had the same heft. The Doomsday angle feels like it's been bolted on to beef up the Brainiac story, a feeling reinforced by the way it's eventually resolved, as an afterthought. Many other DC characters make an appearance. Batman, Steel, Lana and Wonder Woman come across very well, and it's interesting to see the ways that different artists cope with the shame of having to draw Supergirl in her current costume! They cover it up with her cape, draw her from the waist up, or lengthen the sides to turn it into more of a jumpsuit, which is a big improvement. We don't get to see much of the new young Superman's personality in this book, what with the Doomsday infection and everything, but his costume looks weirdly unbalanced without the red underpants. *Stephen Theaker*

★★★☆☆

Films

The Cobbler, by Tom McCarthy and Paul Sado (Voltage Pictures and others)

Max Simkin has been struggling since his dad left, a long time ago now. He's angry at the guy for going, a feeling not helped by going to work each day in the shoe repair shop where his father worked, as well as his grandfather and great-grandfather. Max's mother suffers from dementia, and her well-meaning suggestions to take a nice girl out just drive home the point that all the nice girls he used to know have been married for fifteen years with children. A change in his life is provoked by the appearance in his shop of an obnoxious and aggressive criminal, played by Method Man of the Wu-Tang Clan, who doesn't want the shop to close till he's got his shoes. Max's cobbling machine breaks down and because of the urgency he goes down into the basement and gets out an old machine – a magical machine! He discovers that when he uses it to stitch the soles of a pair of shoes, he turns into a replica of the person to whom they belong. With interesting consequences! Max is played by Adam Sandler, totally convincing in the role of this disappointed, miserable man who doesn't resent his mother for a minute. The friendly barber next door is played by Steve Buscemi, extremely likeable in the role. The film sets out very clearly (though unobtrusively) the rules of the premise: he looks like the person as they look right now (even if they are dead), he takes on their voice and accent, he has to wear both shoes, and they must fit his size ten and a half feet.

Though I liked the film overall, a few things bugged me. The music tries a bit hard, and Max takes off his shoes in some very daft situations, places, for example, where he wouldn't want to leave fingerprints. It feels like that's because we might otherwise go long stretches of the film without seeing its star. Max also seems unbelievably unconcerned about the real-world consequences for the people he impersonates. Fair enough when it's a gangster, but putting on the shoes of a young teenager or a woman and using them to talk to that gangster? That was appalling. The trailer put me off by making it look like Max would use the shoes to impersonate men to have sex with their girlfriends; while still very unwelcome, this plays a tiny part in the film and he doesn't go through with it (albeit because he can't get in the shower without taking off his shoes). The main plot concerns a property developer who wants to get one last tenant out of an old block. As Max disguised himself to help I couldn't help thinking that this was essentially the same plot as the *Daredevil* television series. And this film does feel a lot like a television pilot, even if the actors involved give it the heft of a movie. If there isn't a series currently planned, I'm sure it will happen eventually: easy to imagine the cobbler pulling on a new pair of shoes each week and getting involved in a new set of scrapes. *Stephen Theaker* ★★★☆☆

The Gallows, by Travis Cluff and Chris Lofing (Blumhouse Productions and others)

Funny. Tense. Amped up. Still the critics scoff.

Recent critical response to mass market horror films (*It Follows* (2014) being the exception) has been abysmal. Last year, critics erred in bashing the thoroughly entertaining *As Above, So Below*. Once again, they've lambasted an engaging found footage film with a young adult cast. This time, it's *The Gallows*, and once again, they got it wrong.

The Gallows, directed by Travis Cluff and Chris Lofing, traps four Nebraskan students in a haunted high school performing arts centre. It keeps the viewer locked in from the appalling accident in the first scene until the final twist. At the end of the 81-minute film, I felt as if I'd downed a couple of energy drinks.

Reese has quit his high school football team to pursue the performing arts. His decision is driven solely by his secret crush on Pfeifer, whose acting (versus cheerleading) leanings make her forbidden by Reese's ex-teammate and friend Ryan Shoos. Somehow, Reese has been cast in the male lead – he's a terrible actor – beside Pfeifer in a play that bears the same title of this film.

But there is a far more dangerous threat to Reese: twenty years earlier, Charlie Grimille, slated to play the executioner in the same play, had to step in as the lead. A freak accident during a performance killed Charlie, who is rumoured to haunt the facility.

The loquacious Ryan convinces Reese that the way to avoid bombing his performance (and disappointing Pfeifer) is by destroying the set. Then Reese can swoop in and aid the ailing Pfeifer. So the two young men, accompanied by Reese's snarky girlfriend Cassidy, sneak into the theatre at night, where they encounter Pfeifer. The foursome gets locked in, and thus begins their increasingly horrific escapade.

If you're a "that could never happen" kind of person, perhaps this isn't the film for you. For instance, you'll have to overlook the unlikelihood that a school would repeat the same ill-fated play twenty years later (hey, I didn't say this film was perfect). However, if you can suspend disbelief and stop thinking for an hour and twenty minutes, then go see *The Gallows*. Squirm as the camera lingers on dark passageways, passes through creepy shop rooms, or zooms in on strange objects. Breathe faster amid the creaks and bangs, and feel the tension as an unseen presence grows closer.

If you're willing to plunk down the $10 to $15 to see this film in a cinema with a superior audio-visual system, do it. It adds to the authenticity of scenes, such as that during which the camera view moves along wooden ceiling slats and the thump of footsteps grows louder. During that moment, you are there with those students.

One way this film stands apart from other recent found footage entries is the level of humour, mainly at the beginning. It's driven largely by egocentric and uber-chatty lead cameraman Ryan. In the funniest scene, Ryan steps out from behind the camera, then tosses a football that knocks over a classmate he refers to as "Stage Boy".

Sure, this film probably has a short shelf life, but so

does a good pair of running shoes. And who says a
movie has to have a long shelf life to be enjoyable?
Douglas J. Ogurek ★★★★☆

**The Maze Runner, by Noah Oppenheim,
Grant Pierce Myers and T.S. Nowlin
(Twentieth Century Fox)**

Three years ago Alby (played by Aml Ameen) woke up
in a wooded glade surrounded by immense walls, with
no memory of who he was or how he got there. He
remembered his name after a day or two, but that was
it. Each month another boy arrived in the freight
elevator, bringing with them some essential supplies,
and though it got really bad at times a peaceful
community slowly developed with a few simple rules,
don't hurt each other, and, unless you're a runner,
don't go through the huge gap that opens up in the
wall each morning and closes at night, because if
you're stuck in the maze on the other side when night
falls, and the maze starts to shift, you won't ever come
back.

   The film begins when Thomas (Dylan O'Brien)
arrives. By then there are about thirty-two young men
living in the glade, going by the cast list, and many
others have already died (perhaps they were being
vague with the talk of three years, and maybe there
were months when more than one boy arrived).
Thomas isn't the kind of guy who's happy to chill out
in a lovely, peaceful glade. No, he wants to get out into
the maze and find a way out. Problem is, out there in
the maze live the Grievers, immense spider-cyborgs
who'll kill you just for being in their labyrinth. Gally
(Will Poulter) thinks they should stay where they are
and get on with living their lives. He's totally right and
the main character is an idiot.

   The Maze Runner is a well-produced film, with good

performances from a lot of talented young actors, but it has a lot of story problems. There is very little maze running, for a start, and it's over an hour into the film before it begins. The maze was fully explored before our hero ever turned up, and he just leads a couple of short expeditions before getting very lucky. The maze is supposed to be a trial, a test, but for most of the young men that trial has involved a long, pleasant camping trip in a leafy field with bonfires and bacon. The only people who face any danger are those who fancy it. It could have been more aptly entitled *The Guy Who Lives in a Nice Field with a Bunch of Dudes and Sometimes Pokes Around in the Maze for a Few Minutes*. As part of their brainwashing it seems that the young men have been wiped clean of any desire, since the arrival of a young woman is greeted by many with dismay, as a bad sign. It's not even suggested that her presence might be dangerous because they'll begin to fight over her, or any thought given to what the presence of a woman might mean for the future of their colony. Do they not want to hear the noise of little runners' feet? The monsters are well-designed, but as so often with CGI your heart knows it's not real and they fail to truly thrill. Not an awful film, though, and it's good to see this kind of revelatory science fiction on screen. It's been compared to *The Hunger Games* a lot, but it's much more like a little league version of the Riverworld saga. *Stephen Theaker*
★★★☆☆

Pixels, by Tim Herlihy and Timothy Dowling (1492 Pictures and others)

Alien invasion comedy resurrects classic video games in all their pixelated glory.

Centipede. Donkey Kong. Asteroids. Pac-Man. Most of us who grew up in the eighties did battle with these icons. The video games, with their graphic primitiveness and single screen action, reflect a simpler time... a time of striped socks pulled up to the knees, big hair bands with mind-numbing lyrics, and backyard or field-down-the-road sports.

Pixels, directed by Chris Columbus, brings the ultimate eighties intellect (i.e. Adam Sandler) to the screen with a straightforward objective (i.e. save the world), a plot as simple as a yellow circle munching dots, and an outcome as predictable as the first level in a classic video game. It has a middle school mentality, and it's a blast!

Aliens vs. Nerds

1982 world video game champion hopeful Sam Brenner (Sandler) has become a disillusioned employee ("I'm just a loser who was good at old video games") of the Nerd Brigade, a technology installation/repair company that forces its employees to wear humiliating orange uniforms. His life seems a disappointment, until aliens threaten the earth with gigantic versions of those beloved eighties video game characters. How's that for a concept?!

The aliens, using modified video footage of eighties legends ranging from Daryl Hall and John Oates to *Fantasy Island*'s Mr Roarke and Tattoo, challenge earthlings to a series of video game competitions.

Lifelong friend Will Cooper (Kevin James), now the charmingly bumbling President (of the United States!) pleads with Brenner to reboot his long-dormant gaming skills to resist the aliens. So Brenner and a couple of cartoonish sidekicks set out to save the world. They will fall in love, take outrageous risks, and best of all, lavish the viewer with the triumphant feeling that comes when nerds prevail.

Adam Sandler typically plays one of two roles: the lovable goofball (e.g. *The Waterboy*, *Happy Gilmore*,

Billy Madison) or the down-to-earth good guy (e.g. *Mr Deeds*, *50 First Dates*). In *Pixels*, it's the latter, and it makes sense with an "event film" like this. Moreover, Brenner's "Arcader" allies are more than enough to compensate for Sandler's toned down lead.

First, there's "Wonder Boy" Ludlow Lamonsoff (Josh Gad), a conspiracy theorist who lives with his grandmother and longs to win the love of blonde bombshell Lady Lisa. Ludlow has his work cut out for him, since Lady Lisa is a video game character. Then there's Eddie "The Fire Blaster" Plant (Peter Dinklage), a supremely narcissistic former world video game champion serving time for tech crimes. Rounding out the team are the fun-loving President Cooper and Brenner's love interest Violet (Michelle Monaghan).

Playing the Patterns
Pixels repeatedly references the importance of recognizing and acting on the "patterns" within classic video games. Similarly, the film's makers capitalize on recent alien invasion successes: the destruction of universally recognized monuments, the *Independence Day* recklessness of tossing the U.S. President into the fray, the aliens dropping from a mothership for Avengers/Transformers-style all-out urban chaos. *Pixels*, in essence, plays the patterns, and it wins.

Game challenges pair special effects – ironic, considering the film's graphically archaic muses – with late seventies/early eighties rock anthems. Brenner and Ludlow, accompanied by Loverboy's "Working for the Weekend", blast up at glowing centipedes. Queen's "We Will Rock You" stomps away as Donkey Kong rolls and hurls his digital barrels toward the Arcaders.

Go Guts
When he meets Violet's son Matty, Brenner sarcastically contrasts eighties and contemporary video game experiences. I'm paraphrasing here: "We used to

leave the house and go to these things called arcades. We got together and had fun."

What an apt statement for today's tech-enslaved youth... and adults. *Pixels*, for all its absurdity, encourages viewers to get together and get silly.

In the eighties, our parents didn't enroll us in a dozen different activities. We had to invent our own fun within the confines of our neighbourhoods. And we didn't have Rotten Tomatoes telling us whether or not we should like a film. All we had were our own guts, and with *Pixels*, my gut tells me I want to play again. *Douglas J. Ogurek* ★★★★★

Terminator Genisys, by Laeta Kalogridis and Patrick Lussier (Paramount)

Tirmynator Genisys: the best misspelling since slyced bred.

Yes, let's start with the obvious gripe: *Genisys*. Originally the film was titled *Genesis*, then someone made the executive decision (absolute power corrupting absolutely) to change/distort/pervert it, presumably working under the delusion that misspelling something makes it stand out in a *good* way. One wonders how the original Terminator would have fared had Sarah Connor been misspelled in Skynet's records. The T-1000 would have opened up the phone directory and had a meltdown. *Where is S'air-a Conher? Target cannot be acquired.* And why? (We bang our heads against the nearest busborne billboard.) Why subscribe to this wanton degradation of language? The only explanation that doesn't leave the producers hanging their heads in shame is that the alphabetic disparity between *Genesis* and *Genisys* is intended to mirror the narrative disparity between the events of the first *Terminator* movie and their retrofitting in this latest offering. In which case, well played... but a propensity for randomising still seems the more likely cause! Watch out for *Terminator 6*, where Skynet, unable to destroy humanity by conventional means, sends a T-3000 back to 12 May 1754 to kill Samuel Johnson. Without his dictionary to unite them, the Resistance of the future is torn apart by wilful misspellings.

The Terminator (1984) and *Terminator 2: Judgment*

Day (1991) were near perfect films, whose cult appeal gave rise to a cinematic catch-22: fans desperately craved more, yet no escalation was possible; the only way to avoid the disappointment of absence was to fill it with disappointment. Thus we were given *Terminator 3: Rise of the Machines* (2003) and *Terminator Salvation* (2009), neither of which failed to float post-drowning to the surface of low expectations. For all that viewers might have hoped, thematically there was just nowhere for these sequels to go. Without any form of progression, all that remained was nostalgia. By the time the closing credits rolled, the verdict in both cases was that nostalgia could better be sought by re-watching the originals! Yet, the conundrum remained: how to satisfy the cult craving for more Terminator when the first two films already had achieved everything the genre could offer. *Terminator Genisys* supplies the obvious answer: change genres.

   The movie begins as if it is nothing more than a remake of James Cameron's first film, dumbed down slightly and slicked up to allow for thirty years' worth of devolution within the industry. This, however, proves not to be the case. As 1984 is recreated and *The Terminator* begins to play out again, suddenly, playfully, the expected events are subverted and *Terminator Genisys* breaks free of its lineage, reinventing itself as an action comedy. It's a creative decision that no doubt will outrage Terminator purists just as much as films three and four's inability to recapture the emotional effect of their predecessors. Arnie had to be incorporated, so his iconic T-1000 is allowed to age like Schwarzenegger himself. The paradox element of Skynet versus John and Sarah Connor had become so complex as to evolve into an independent lifeform capable of defying both continuity and genuine fear for the future. Solution:

treat this aspect with tongue-in-cheek flippancy. Thus, Terminators are no longer a source of nightmares; but what *Genisys* lacks in cold menace and the adrenaline of relentless pursuit, it makes up for (at least to some extent) by being *enjoyable*. This doesn't make it a classic – there can never *be* another Terminator classic – but it does afford the movie a *raison d'être*, and hence a legitimacy, that *Rise of the Machines* and *Salvation* lacked. Yes, the camera has to be discreet in not showing up how short Emilia Clarke's Sarah Connor is compared to Linda Hamilton's. True, there are motivations that defy reason and plot points left deliberately without explanation. But whereas this would demand censure in SF suspense (and from those who believe they should be watching such), in action comedy the deficiencies can be plastered over with humour.

Even within this genre, of course, *Terminator Genisys* is not without its faults. After all, we are living in a future where CGI technology came online and wiped out all but a handful of good filmmakers. Please, would somebody send a message back through time and warn them: any action sequence that could not be achieved *without* CGI is not going to be exciting *with* it, capisce? Computer game helicopters? Olympic gymnast buses? Nobody can be expected to take a Terminator seriously as a killing machine when anyone it sets its sights on immediately becomes impervious to injury by any other means. But at least this isn't the crux of the film. *Terminator Genisys* really does play on the humorous potential of the scenario, and for those who might raise a sceptical eyebrow, look no further than J.K. Simmons' portrayal of Detective O'Brien, who as a rookie was caught up in the carnage of 1984 and thirty years on is still obsessing over what he witnessed, a subject of ridicule for his highflying, unimaginative young colleagues. Okay, that doesn't actually sound particularly funny on paper, but on screen, in the moment, it works.

And if you buy into the film's exuberance less as a critical advocate of Terminators I and II and more as someone who finds release in the madness (O'Brien: "I know what's going on here has to be really, really complicated." Sarah Connor: "We're here to stop the end of the world." O'Brien: "I can work with that.") then so too does *Terminator Genisys*... regardless of how it's spelt. *Jacob Edwards*

Games

Rare Replay, by Rare (Microsoft Studios)

When I bought the Xbox One, I never imagined – or dared to dream! – that one day I would use it to play *Atic Atac*. But sometimes dreams come true, even the ones you never dreamt! *Rare Replay* is a collection of thirty of Rare's games, going all the way back to their days as the fabled gods of ZX Spectrum, Ultimate Play the Game. Their name was a guarantee of quality in those days where the hottest new titles would cost just £5.50. The oldest game here is the evergreen *Jetpac*, still as good as ever. A few titles at either end of the Spectrum era don't make the cut – like *Psst!*, *Trans Am* and *Alien 8* – and one can only hope that DLC will be forthcoming, but the stone cold classics are, like *Lunar Jetman*, still as rock hard as ever, till you realise this collection adds a rewind button that turns you into Tom Cruise in *Edge of Tomorrow*, magically anticipating enemies before they even materialise. It never occurred to me, playing that game thirty years ago, that there might be so many more aliens in the game than I had ever seen. Destroying one alien base still feels like a great achievement, but with the rewind

button in play I managed eight! Then there are the games that dared to cost ten pounds: *Sabre Wulf*, rope-swinging *Underworlde* and isometric werewolf adventure *Knight Lore*, and the less fun *Gunfright* which still impresses by replacing the traditional "rooms" with a scrolling three-dimensional environment. Ultimate then became Rare, and began to produce games for Nintendo, games that were always out of my price range. I was still playing on my Spectrum the day I saw *WipEout* and the PlayStation on *Gamesmaster* with Patrick Moore! So there are several titles here that are completely new to me:

Battletoads, *Slalom*, *Blast Corps*, *Killer Instinct*, and most excitingly (for me at least) *Solar Jetman*, which turns out to be a clone of *Thrust*, albeit with enough new features to make it well worth playing. Some of their notable games from this period are inevitably missing, for rights reasons, like *Donkey Kong Country* and *Goldeneye*. Others, like *Perfect Dark* and *Banjo-Kazooie*, appear in the form of their Xbox 360 remakes, produced after Rare became part of Microsoft. Rather than being part of the *Rare Replay* game proper (at least in the digital version), these are downloaded to the Xbox One in their Xbox 360 versions, and can be run separately too. (It doesn't look like they become part of your Xbox 360 library, though, which is a shame.) Here too are the Xbox 360 originals, like *Kameo: Elements of Power*, *Perfect Dark Zero*, *Viva Pinata* and *Jetpac Refuelled*, all a bit underappreciated upon their original release but sure to find their fans now. I love that *Perfect Dark Zero* includes a bot multiplayer mode; I wish more games did. From the fact that I've written quite a lot of review without saying a great deal about any of the individual games, and not even mentioning half of them, you can tell what a huge package this is. I've barely scratched the surface, both here and while playing it. I haven't yet mentioned the special features that can be unlocked, or the snapshots that let you play strangely altered versions of those classic Spectrum games (*Underworlde* without the creatures!), the ten thousand gamer points (there is an achievement just for playing most of the games!), or the price: amazingly, it costs just twenty pounds. *Rare Replay* is an essential purchase for Xbox One owners, and goes a long way towards making the Xbox One an essential purchase too. It's an instant games collection, and they are some of the best games ever made. *Stephen Theaker* ★★★★★

Saints Row IV: Re-Elected, by Volition Software (Deep Silver)

An Xbox One re-release of the lovably reprehensible Xbox 360 game, including two expansions, Enter the Dominatrix and How the Saints Saved Christmas, this picks up in gameplay terms from where the *Saints Row: The Third* expansions went: superpowers. Jumping over (small) buildings in a single bound, almost as fast as a speeding bullet, and throwing blasts of ice and fire like Spider-Man's amazing friends. When the game begins you are president of the United States of America, and Keith David is vice-president. Luckily the tedium of governing the nation is broken by an alien invasion, who abduct you and your staff and at least some of the human race before blowing up the planet and sticking you all in a computer simulation of your home town. Yes, this series may have begun as a cheap knock-off of *Grand Theft Auto* but it's carved out territory of its very own in the places other grown-up games don't go: the ludicrous, the unrealistic, the absurd, the capricious. It's post-modern, metatextual, and constantly self-referential. The Enter the Dominatrix expansion, for example, is presented as a series of deleted scenes from the main game, with the characters from the game commenting on their portrayal in the scenes and their performances, and climactic sequences shown as pre-vis rather than expensive cut-scenes. There are aspects I don't much like: search for the game on Google Images and you're likely to see unflattering snapshots of strippers, bondage gear and giant dildo bats. However, the option to customise your main character means that this can be (and was for me) a game about the amazing brown-skinned female president who saved humanity. While wearing nifty costumes, like a pirate suit or a superhero costume or pretty much anything else you can think of, up to and including a giant Barack Obama head. And then she makes friends with a race of dinosaurs! This may not ever be a series of games that I'll buy on release day, but when the DLC is bundled in and you can get it for a good price it becomes an essential purchase. There is a deep well of nonsensical fun and intelligent idiocy here that other games would do well to draw on. The item I'd like to take from this game into others: the Christmas dubstep gun, that makes everyone bounce around to a Yuletide jingle. *Stephen Theaker* ★★★★☆

Music

It Follows: Original Motion Picture Soundtrack, by Disasterpeace (Milan Records)

This eighteen-track album collects the score from the film *It Follows*, directed by David Robert Mitchell, about a young woman infected by a supernatural curse. As with the film, there are strong echoes of John Carpenter's early work in this electronic music, especially in tracks like "Title" and "Playpen", while moody tracks like "Anyone" and "Detritus" will appeal to those who enjoyed the eeriness of Aphex Twin's *Selected Ambient Works, Volume 2*, but it's an imaginative work of electronic music in its own right. I bought the album before seeing the film, and it stands alone very well. Watching the film makes it even better. On screen the music is used to create an uncanny sense of derangement in the viewer, its jarring strangeness accentuating the horror, and delicious echoes of that carry across to subsequent listens to the soundtrack. *Stephen Theaker* ★★★★☆

Television

Daredevil, Season 1, by Drew Goddard and chums (Marvel/Netflix)

Matt Murdock is a blind lawyer affronted by the injustice he sees in his home of Hell's Kitchen, a part of New York damaged badly in the battle between the Avengers and Loki's army of alien invaders. Property developers are moving in, but some of the current inhabitants don't want to move out, and that's the kind of case that the newly established firm of Nelson and Murdock can be persuaded to take. What the two lawyers don't know at first is that behind it all is a shadowy kingpin, who is bringing together Russian, Chinese and Japanese gangsters in one great criminal enterprise. Anyone who dares to utter his name – Wilson Fisk – is killed for their indiscretion, making it impossible to pin anything on him. It would be an impossible situation were it not for Matt's unusual abilities. The chemicals that took his sight enhanced all his other senses – taste, touch, hearing and balance – and he was trained in combat, at least for a time, by the mysterious Stick. These skills let Matt fight for the city, at first in a black mask, and by the end of the series in the distinctive red suit of Marvel's Daredevil.

This is an extremely violent series, much more so than *Agents of SHIELD* or *Agent Carter*, not suitable at all for children. Matt Murdock tends to get very badly wounded, since he's often fighting against the odds. A fight in the second episode is the best I've ever seen on television, like looking down the classic corridor scene in *Oldboy*. Wilson Fisk is an utterly brutal villain, his fists the piledrivers they are in the comics, Vincent D'Onofrio's performance so chilling, so physical and intense, that he'd have had awards nominations if this wasn't a series about a superhero. (I hope we'll see him face off against the Avengers or Spider-Man or Daredevil himself on the big screen at some point.) It draws on many periods of the comics, in particular those written by Frank Miller, Brian Michael Bendis and Mark Waid, to create a classic version of the character. The mood is dingy and grim, though Foggy brings just the right amount of humour to stop it getting too gruelling – and were those the stilts of Stilt-Man I saw in the background of one scene? Its pace is very much its own; this couldn't be a network show, with the constant need to cue up adverts that has made programmes like *The Big Bang Theory* little more than a series of vignettes. The episodes stretch out fully over their running length, building up to moments of sudden, shocking violence. My only grumble is about the frequent discussions about the existence or not of god (Matt Murdock being a Catholic and Wilson Fisk an atheist), which seem bizarre given that the season's plot follows on from a battle between Loki and Thor. Would people keep believing in other gods, or for that matter remain atheists, when real gods have been seen on television? Perhaps they would, but it makes Matt seem a bit daft. But that's just a minor issue. I wouldn't just rate this higher than the other Marvel television series, I'd rate it higher than most of the movies. And season two is going to feature the Punisher and Elektra! Let's hope a change of showrunner doesn't put a billy club in the works. *Stephen Theaker* ★★★★☆

Game of Thrones, Season 5, by David Benioff, D.B. Weiss and chums (Sky Atlantic)

Tyrion crosses the sea in a crate, reluctantly, to start a new life working for Daenyrs, the mother of dragons. She's having trouble keeping control of her city, the previous ruling class refusing to accept the changes she has made. Jon Snow and the men of the Night's

Watch must consider what to do with the defeated
Wildlings. Winter is coming, and if humanity doesn't
stand together, even the scruffy ones with bad hair,
they'll all be killed by the zombie army of the White
Walkers. And then be revived to join that army!
Winterfell suffers under the heel of a mad tyrant,
while further south King's Landing falls prey to
religious mania. Elsewhere, Arya learns what it takes
to become an assassin like the Faceless Man. This is
probably the weakest season of the programme so far,
and the level of violence towards women and children
is extremely uncomfortable at times. But it's still very
good. By now we care about these characters; we've
watched some of them grow up, we've seen what
they've been through, and their lives matter to us. The
effects are of a very high quality. The Wildling giant, in
particular, is magnificent. *Stephen Theaker* ★★★☆☆

Penny Dreadful, Season 2, by John Logan and chums (Sky Atlantic)

A coven of (often naked) witches is determined to
bring Vanessa Ives to meet their master, and they have
identified lonely Sir Malcolm Murray, so much in need
of comfort after the events of season one, as a weak
point in the Penny Dreadful gang. Meanwhile, Doctor
Frankenstein makes the mistake of falling in love with
the bride his creature has demanded, and Dorian Grey
shows how romantic he can be. Ethan Chandler has a
particularly hairy time of it in these episodes, but his
relationship with Vanessa Ives deepens, particularly
during a short break in her holiday cottage at the
coast. The reverse of season one, this run starts slowly
but ends well. The blood and gore continues at a level
appropriate for a programme with this title. The
announcers on Sky Atlantic typically warn that viewers
may find some scenes disturbing, but there are scenes
in this series that only a psychopath would *not* find

disturbing. And yet there is noticeably more smiling this time around, even from tortured souls Ethan and Vanessa, perhaps to alleviate the bleakness. Eva Green as Vanessa is once again the star of the show. While the other characters, at least in the early episodes, feel rather like a league of boring gentlemen, she looks like she was drawn by Kevin O'Neill and brings Mark Hamill levels of belief and commitment to every scene. *Stephen Theaker* ★★★☆☆

Under the Dome, Season 1, by Brian K. Vaughan and chums (Amazon Instant Video)

An invisible force field materialises around and over a small town, trapping everyone inside its dome, and keeping everyone else out. There are immediate tragedies as trucks, cars and aircraft smash into it, and one poor cow gets sliced in two. (And oh how sick you get of seeing it get bisected, since the shot is included in every subsequent "Previously...") Some of the town's most prominent citizens have been up to no good, albeit in a way that leaves it with enough propane to keep the lights on, and that makes it necessary for strong-arm debt collector Barbie to get more involved in keeping the town safe than he'd like. That's made all the more awkward by him getting into a relationship with the wife of one of his previous customers. Others trapped inside include a pair of teenagers who begin to have dome-given visions, another girl with a dangerously obsessive boyfriend, and that boyfriend's father, Big Jim, the rock on which the town relies. Can the people of this town survive each other long enough to survive the dome? Possibly not, given the townsfolks' peculiar habit of declaring their intentions to go to the police to the very people they suspect of foul play. The viewer's hands will frequently be thrown in the air in disbelief. Overall, this was a disappointment. I hadn't read the Stephen King novel on which it is based, but there are few adaptations of his work I haven't enjoyed – this comes in at the lower end of those. The mysteries of the dome provide a few jaw-dropping moments, but they're wedded to crime and corruption stories from a third-rate *Justified* imitation. If this hadn't been renewed, the ending of the season would have been an incredible letdown. (Spoiler: the dome changes colour. Well, there's more to it that that, you find out in season two, but not a lot.) It's at its best showing how fragile our grip on life can be, especially for those who need medical support, at its worst when it forgets that its better-hearted characters would be sure to tell each what they know about the killers and maniacs hiding in plain sight. It's not awful, but there is lots of room in the dome for improvement. *Stephen Theaker* ★★★☆☆

Notes

Also Received, But Not Yet Reviewed
Notes by Stephen Theaker

Connell, Brendan, *Cannibals of West Papua* (Zagava)
De Abaitua, Matthew, *If Then* (Angry Robot): reviewed for *Interzone* #261.
De La Haye, Joan, *Burning* (Fox Spirit Books)
Hughes, Rhys, *Mirrors in the Deluge* (Elsewhen Press)
Hurley, Andrew Michael, *The Loney* (John Murray): now received in hardback.
Kewin, Simon, *Engn* (December House)
Kewin, Simon, *Hedge Witch* (Stormcrow Books)
McQuay, Alec, *Spares* (Fox Spirit Books)
Savile, Steven, *King Wolf* (Fox Spirit Books)
Sigurdardottir, Yrsa, *The Undesired* (Hodder & Stoughton): translation by Victoria Cribb.
Warom, Ren, *The Lonely Dark* (Fox Spirit Books)

About TQF

Copyright

ISBN (print): 978-1-910387-11-5
ISBN (epub): 978-1-910387-12-2

ISSN (print): 1747-6083
ISSN (online): 1747-6075

Website: www.theakersquarterly.blogspot.com

Email: theakersquarterlyfiction@gmail.com

Lulu Store: www.lulu.com/silveragebooks

Feedbooks: www.feedbooks.com/userbooks/tag/tqf

Submissions: Submissions are very welcome! See website for guidelines and terms.

Advertising: We welcome ad swaps with small press publishers and other creative types, and we'll run ads for relevant new projects from former contributors.

Sending material for review: We are interested in reviewing almost anything that's fantasy-related. We prefer to receive books for review in epub or mobi format. Feel free to send ebooks without querying first. We have reviewed about 14% of items received, though many of those reviewed are things we've actively requested from places like NetGalley.

Mission statement: The primary goal of *Theaker's Quarterly Fiction* is to keep going. If you're wondering why we do something a particular way, our primary goal is probably why.

respective authors, who have assumed all responsibility for any legal problems arising from publication of their material. Other material copyright Stephen Theaker and John Greenwood.

Published in Theaker's Paperback Library on 15 January 2016.

Our Other Publications

Theaker's Quarterly Fiction #1–52
Stephen Theaker and John Greenwood (eds)

Space University Trent: Hyperparasite
Walt Brunston

There Are Now a Billion Flowers
The Hatchling (forthcoming)
John Greenwood

The Mercury Annual
Pilgrims at the White Horizon
Michael Wyndham Thomas

The Conan Doyle Weirdbook
Rafe McGregor (ed.)

Professor Challenger in Space
Quiet, the Tin Can Brains Are Hunting!
The Fear Man
Howard Phillips in His Nerves Extruded
Howard Phillips and The Doom That Came to Sea Base Delta
Howard Phillips and The Day the Moon Wept Blood
Stephen Theaker

Five Forgotten Stories
John Hall

Elephant
Harsh Grewal

Elsewhere
Steven Gilligan

New Words #1–4
John Greenwood, Steven Gilligan
and Stephen Theaker (eds)

Forthcoming Attractions

Expect **Theaker's Quarterly Fiction #54**
sometime soon!

Our blog is rather more active now:
www.theakersquarterly.blogspot.com

Stephen tweets every few days or so at:
www.twitter.com/Rolnikov

The zine now has its own Twitter account too:
www.twitter.com/TheakersQrtly

Our email address is:
theakersquarterlyfiction@gmail.com

www.ingramcontent.com/pod-product-compliance
Lightning Source LLC
Chambersburg PA
CBHW060620130626
46555CB00002B/591